NEMORAMA THE NAUTCHNEE

NEMORAMA THE NAUTCHNEE

A STORY OF INDIA

EDWIN MACMINN

GYAN

Published by

GYAN

Gyan Publishing House
5, Ansari Road
Daryaganj, New Delhi-110002
Phone: 011-47034999, 9811692060
E-mail: books@gyanbooks.com

Distribution Network
gyanbooks.com
India, USA, Canada, UK, Australia

ISBN: 978-93-7014-212-1 (PB)

First Published, 1890

2nd Impression 2025

Printed at: Gyan Press, Delhi.

NEMORAMA THE NAUTCHNEE

Arthur EDWIN MACMINN

OUTWARD BOUND.

NEMORAMA THE NAUTCHNEE

A STORY OF INDIA

BY REV. EDWIN MacMINN

JERSEY CITY, NEW JERSEY

AUTHOR OF

Breaker Boy, *Eaglesmere Trio*, *Brave Hearts Win*, *Judith and Glaucia*, *Ben Ammi*, *Bushkill Social*, *Amal the Amalekite*, *A German Hero*, *Rambles in Mineral Fields*, *The Crystal Club*, *From Cave to Palace*, *Pocket Manual No. 3*, etc.

1890

DEDICATED

TO THE

WOMEN'S FOREIGN MISSIONARY SOCIETIES IN AMERICA,

WHOSE RECOGNITION OF THE SISTERHOOD OF THEIR SEX IN ALL THE WORLD HAS LED THEM TO CONSECRATE THEIR PRAYERS, GIFTS, AND LABOR TO THE SOCIAL ELEVATION AND ETERNAL SALVATION OF THOSE NOW BOUND BY THE CASTE CUSTOM OF BRAHMANISM;

WHOSE WORK

IS A RECOGNITION OF THE CALL OF

THEIR DIVINE MASTER

TO GO FORTH, AS DID MARY, AND ANNOUNCE THE GLAD TIDINGS OF A RISEN LORD, AND TO CARRY TO THE CITIES OF HEATHENISM; AS DID PHŒBE THE EPISTLE TO ROME, THE TRIUMPHANT DOCTRINES OF SALVATION.

PREFACE.

THIS story has been written to aid the Woman's Foreign Missionary Societies in arousing the members of our churches to a greater zeal in their special work. The history given seemed necessary as a foundation for understanding why things are as they are in India. The history, customs, descriptions, etc., are prepared with great care to truly represent the state of the case.

It is with the hope that we may have more sympathy for our earnest, struggling missionaries that this book is sent forth. They are noble, cultured men and women of God, and we too often forget how much their success is laid upon our shoulders by the Lord of all.

While writing this story I had the pleasure of entertaining Ramabai at my house, and her eyes sparkled with appreciation of my effort as I told her of my purpose. And now I send it forth with the fond hope that it may do some good by arousing in many souls enthusiasm for zenana missions.

EDWIN MCMINN.

CONTENTS.

NEMORAMA THE NAUTCHNEE.

CHAPTER I.

CALLED TO BE A MISSIONARY.

SYLVIA, one of the prettiest towns in the Keystone State, was said to contain, in proportion to its population, a larger number of attractive maidens than any other town in the State.

There seemed to be a limited supply of young men, and this naturally induced the young ladies to be more gracious and entertaining than they might have been had the inequality been reversed. This condition of affairs also had the tendency to encourage the young men to magnify their own importance. Some of them were vain enough to think that one man was as good as four women, which is true Mohammedan doctrine. This was too much for the maidens to endure. They vehemently asserted their individual equality, and proved it by their broader culture and greater skill. They ranked higher in their classes at school, were better clerks in the stores, more efficient as stenographers and typewriters, and more reliable in the work of the Church. In a small cottage in this village lived the widow Thompson and her three daughters. Her life seemed to have more than its share of trials, but, from her sunny face and bright home, one would have thought she was a stranger to care and sadness.

Many years previous her husband died, leaving her without property and with three little daughters to support. The widow knew how to ply her needle, and she went diligently to work. The years passed on; the home was preserved, the children clothed, fed, and educated. When the streaks of silver lighted upon the handsome head of the mother the daughters took up the burdens, and bore them for her. One was a school-teacher, one a stenographer, and the remaining one—having just returned from a ladies' college with the honors of her class—was ready to go whither the Lord should lead her.

Jennie Thompson was one of the most handsome and winning of her sex. With a mind of broad culture, a voice of exquisite sweetness, a form of perfect symmetry, and movements of polished grace she attracted every one; but, by the sympathy of her heart and the consecration of her soul to God, she held the most powerful sway over her adorers.

The pastor of the church was a frequent visitor at this delightful home, for here he found sympathy with his progressive plans, and ardent co-operation in carrying them forward. Here he beheld the grace of womanhood and felt the exalting influence of noble lives. In the work of the church a Woman's Foreign Missionary Society had been organized. It was yet in its infancy, but every month the zeal of its members was stirred by fresh news from the foreign field. The missionary secretary in charge of the mission work of the State had been a missionary in Burmah, but was compelled by broken health to return home. His eloquent appeals for missions awakened the hearts of his own people, and thus he accomplished the work to which he believed God had called him. In seeking to aid this band of noble workers, and to incite them to greater zeal, he suggested that they invite Ramabai to lecture for them.

The pastor called at the widow's cottage to see what she thought about it. When he had read the letter from the secretary Jennie asked, as she continued the fancy knitting she was engaged in, "Who is Ramabai?"

The pastor responded: "I can very fully answer you, Jennie, for I have just read the story of her life in a book called *The High Caste Hindu Woman*, which Ramabai has published.

"In the Mangalore district of western India was born Ananta Shastri, of high caste parentage. When ten years of age he was married, and his child-bride was brought to his mother's house and committed to her keeping to learn the duties of a high caste Hindu's wife. Ananta was possessed with a desire for knowledge, and, consequently, left his home to obtain instruction from a learned pundit in Poona. This eminent Brahman was employed by the reigning peshwa to visit his palace at stated times and give lessons in Sanskrit to his favorite wife. Ananta, being only a boy, was given the privilege of accompanying his teacher to the palace, and here he occasionally heard the noble lady reciting Sanskrit poems. He was filled with wonder that a woman should be so learned; his admiration was awakened, and he resolved to teach his wife, that she also might possess the graces of learning. With a finished education at the age of twenty-three, he returned to his home and began instructing his wife, but she had no desire to be instructed. His mother and all the elders of the family objected to such an unusual procedure, and he was compelled to relinquish his project.

"In a few years his wife died and he went on a pilgrimage.

"One morning a man on a religious pilgrimage with his wife and two daughters was resting in a village on the banks of the sacred river Godavari. While bathing in the river he noticed a fine-looking man with the same caste tokens also bathing there. After their ablutions and morning prayers he entered into conversation with the stranger. On learning his caste and clan and dwelling-place, and that he was a widower, he offered to him for a wife his little nine-year-old daughter.

"The stranger accepted the offer. The terms of

A BRAHMAN.

the marriage were agreed upon, and the next day the marriage was concluded. The little girl was placed in the possession of the stranger, who took her to his own home, nine hundred miles away. The parents now proceeded on their pilgrimage with light hearts, for they thought they had done their duty to their child. The man who married the little girl was Ananta, and these two became the parents of Ramabai.

"Arriving at his home, Ananta placed the little bride in the hands of his mother to be instructed in wifely duties, and at the same time he began to teach her Sanskrit. But the elders of the family again objected. Ananta determined not to be hindered, so he took his child-bride away from home and the fertile valley in which he had lived, and journeyed into the forest of Gungamul, an extensive jungle on a remote plateau of the western Ghauts.

"The first night spent in the jungle they were without shelter. The little bride, wrapped tight in her cotton quilt, lay upon the ground while Ananta kept watch over her. To add to the terror of the darkness, all night long the cries of a tiger were heard as it roamed about a ravine near by.

"The next day a rude dwelling was constructed, preparations for a food supply were begun, and their solitary life was entered upon. The wild animals of the jungle were all about them, terrifying the child with their wild roaring and crying, but the lessons went on day by day.

"As she grew in years she became wise in the sacred language of her people.

"In a few years children were born to them. The knowledge of this remote dwelling-place of the learned Brahman soon reached the people in the valleys and cities below the mountain, and it became the object of pious pilgrimages, and multitudes of young men flocked to Ananta asking to become his students. Ananta received them with true hospitality until his patrimony was exhausted; then, aged, poor, and blind, he left his forest home, and, with his family, became pilgrims, going from one sacred locality to another. At the time they gave up their home Ramabai was nine years of age. During their pilgrim life her studies were diligently pursued. When she was sixteen years of age her parents died. She continued her pilgrimages with her brother, and lectured on female education.

"After a while her brother died, but she continued her work. In a few months after that she married a Bengali gentleman, but in less than two years he died. She then resumed her lecturing, and, leaving her own country, visited England, and afterward came to America to raise money to establish such schools as would enable her to introduce female education in India."

When the pastor finished his narrative the ladies, with one voice, said, "O yes; by all means, let us have Ramabai address us."

The announcement of so distinguished a speaker was sufficient to crowd the meeting-house long before the appointed hour. In that same place, years before, while the land was bleeding under the strokes of civil war, Anna Dickinson's eloquent appeal had stirred the hearts of the older people. Recently the enthusiasm of the younger folks had been awakened by the thrilling words of Frances E. Willard pleading the cause of temperance. With no less degree of interest they now gazed upon the sweet face of the olive-hued woman who dared to stand opposed to the prejudices of millions of her own people, and plead with their American sisters to labor for their liberation from the chains of ignorance. Ramabai was profoundly touched by the responsive sympathy on the faces of her hearers, and with all the eloquence of her soul told the story of the wrongs under which millions of women in India are to-day suffering. Jennie Thompson was deeply affected by the plea of the eloquent speaker. She could not restrain the tears that sought to flow down her cheeks. And when Ramabai appealed for helpers she felt the inexpressible thrill of a divine call to this field as her life-work.

When the flash of light from God's throne fell upon her she forgot the place where she was, the great audience about her, the exercises following the lecture, and only thought of the millions of India's hosts passing before her.

Ramabai had said, "In India there are 669,100

widows, under twenty years of age, doomed for life to seclusion and suffering. Of these 79,000 are under nine years of age, 207,400 are between the ages of ten and fourteen, 382,700 are between the ages of fifteen and nineteen ; and of all ages and castes there are in India 20,930,600 widows—an army of suffering ones appealing to the hearts of the women of happy America."

Jennie was awakened from her reverie by the people rising to depart. She hastened to her home, and, going to her room, knelt at the spot sacred to her devotions and poured out her soul in consecration to her Saviour. All night long she continued in prayer, and, when morning came, with calm mind and serious countenance announced to her family her acceptance of the call to go and teach the truth of Christ to the daughters of India. With tears and prayers her mother gave her consent, and the work of preparation began.

In a few weeks Jennie entered the Women's Medical College in Philadelphia, where the noble Anandibai Joshee, the first Hindu woman that in any country ever received the degree of doctor of medicine, had been educated. Under influences in thorough sympathy with her purpose Jennie studied medicine and received lessons in Sanskrit. In due time she was graduated, then returned to her home to spend a few weeks before leaving it forever.

That last Sabbath at home was very precious to her

soul. It was the church's communion season, and after the observance of the ordinance the pastor, in touching words, somewhat hindered by flowing tears, committed her as a precious lamb of the flock to the tender mercies of the heavenly Shepherd. The people gathered about her to speak their farewells, each one having a special word of endearment to express. From old and young came the same tribute of love to her and admiration of the noble spirit that enabled her to make this sacrifice. How great it was they could all infer as they recalled Ramabai's words concerning the ignorance and prejudice and caste rules of the women of India. The life of a missionary would be a very lonely life. Only a strong dependence upon God could have enabled the widow Thompson thus to give her daughter to missions. But if God gave his Son to die for mankind should not she sacrifice her natural spirit and give her child to save souls from eternal death? Jennie was a gift laid upon God's altar just as much as was Isaac when laid upon the altar by Abraham, and God gave the widow peace in making the sacrifice.

At length the last farewells were spoken, and Jennie Thompson, accompanied by her pastor, left Sylvia, and in a few hours arrived in New York. Here she entered the great steam-ship *Etruria*, bound for England, and in a few hours the vessel was plowing the waves of the sea. Before retiring Jennie went on deck, and in the distance saw the electric lights of

Asbury Park and Ocean Grove. Taking one last, lingering look at them, she went to her berth. When morning came the vessel was rocking on the waves of the Gulf Stream a hundred miles from the shore. The week on the ocean rapidly passed away, for the passengers were her own countrymen, and their sociability kept lonesomeness away. At Liverpool another vessel was taken for Alexandria, upon which she found as fellow voyagers people of other climes than her own, whose faces, manners, and language were strange and unattractive.

CHAPTER II.

OUTWARD BOUND.

JENNIE realized how thoroughly she was separated from her native land when the vessel passed between the Pillars of Hercules, and plowed the waves of the Mediterranean. An ocean was between her and home.

Her heart grew faint as they neared Egypt, for here she was to leave the vessel at Alexandria, travel overland to Ismaïlia, and embark in another vessel to bear her to India.

Even the sight of pyramids, obelisks, sphynxes, and the peculiar features of Egyptian life failed to restore her courage. A great wave of homesickness rushed overwhelmingly upon her.

At Ismaïlia she boarded the large and elegant steamer *Surat*, a vessel of 3,142 tons' burden, with state-rooms for a hundred and thirty first-class passengers, and a huge crowd of sailors, servants, and steerage passengers, resembling a small army. As she passed up the gang-plank she observed a number of Americans on the deck, and instantly her homesickness vanished. Like a streak of sunshine suddenly released from an intervening cloud the smiles of courage flashed upon her countenance, and she was again filled with hope. When all was ready the great lines were cast off, the engines began their working, the huge vessel swung out into the channel, and then, at the rate of thirteen knots an hour, pursued the way to India.

As they advanced down the Red Sea the heat became so intense, particularly when the breeze was blowing in the same direction the vessel was going, that orders would be occasionally given to reverse the engines, and make a short run against the wind so as to relieve the ship's load of the exhaustion caused by the dead heat of the tropics.

The passengers, clad in thinnest and softest clothing, reclined in easy-chairs under broad awnings on the quarter-deck. Every device to cause the air to be in motion about them was adopted, and, as the evening hours advanced, and the intense heat of the sun abated, the passengers in groups sought to relieve the *ennui* of the journey by games, music, and conversation.

Sociability was one of the characteristics of the travelers, and naturally the various nationalities drew closely to their own people. Jennie was delighted to find two American gentlemen among the passengers, and they, in turn, were equally pleased with the discovery that the lady who tripped up the plank at Ismaïlia was their own countrywoman. During the remainder of the voyage these gentlemen vied with each other, in all the graces of politeness and attention, to make the time pass comfortably and happily to their fair companion. The group attracted much attention from the other passengers, who observed that its uniqueness consisted in its thorough Americanism.

The gentlemen were about the same in age and in size. In some respects they might have passed for brothers, for their general appearance and similarity in disposition were manifest. To have selected one in preference to the other would have called for a closer examination of their characters than a casual glance would have given.

The one most attractive, by a careless, happy, brilliant manner of speech and action, was Edward Morgan, the son of a New York millionaire.

He had recently completed his university course, and was now on a tour of pleasure preliminary to settling down to a life of toil in his father's counting-house. He had distinguished himself in the lecture halls, on the ball ground, and in the boat race. He was a typical educated American, with mind and muscle equally trained, and was looking forward to some vigorous tiger hunting in the vast jungles of India as a sport fitting to his physical capacity.

He had paid a great deal more attention to philosophy than to religion, and was quite familiar with the latest works on theosophy and esoteric Buddhism. Hence, while familiar, as any ordinary church-goer would be, with his home religion, the peculiar transcendentalism of a foreign creed had attracted him to such a degree that even the filthiest fakirs of India would be of great interest to him. Like many of his class, at home he had attended church as a matter of form. When the preacher uttered glittering flights of fancy, or speculated on abstruse questions, he was interested, but when the sober realities of life and death, of obligation and judgment, were broached, he turned his thoughts to more pleasant themes.

He was a thorough gentleman, and never polluted his lips with words of vulgarity or blasphemy, and above all things honored truth and despised a lie. He was the best specimen of a cultured irreligious man Miss Thompson had ever met. He was accustomed to wine-drinking, theater-going, dancing, card-playing, and all the pleasures of high-toned society, and from every form of refined pleasure drew largely to make life a success. He felt strong contempt for the man with so little self-control or will-power as to be overcome by indulgence in any form of pleasure. His own life had been so well ordered that he had never once lost his power of preserving his equipoise. From this superiority to many of his fellows had sprung a spirit of pride, which made him more attractive to the ladies than he would have been with greater humility. His fellow American voyager, with whom he had become acquainted on this vessel, was the Rev. Paul Stanhope, a man in every way his equal.

Paul Stanhope was of Puritan ancestry. For generations the family had prided itself on its purity and zeal for God; how natural, therefore, that the favorite son should consecrate his life to the service of leading men to salvation. His education had been thorough in every particular. In college, university, and theological seminary he had given proof of his superior mental endowment. And frequently upon the rostrum he had shown the possession of brilliant oratorical powers. In any profession he might choose to devote his life he could win honors and emoluments. With strong will-power, he deliberately turned from the pleasures of society, and was now on his way to Benares, the sacred city of the Hindus, to devote his life to humble missionary work. Jennie Thompson keenly felt the spell of his consecrated enthusiasm, and in the society of these brilliant men grew in her views of the sacredness of the talents intrusted to man.

Morgan, separated from his usual companions and brought into such close relations with these missionaries, was profoundly impressed with the sterling spiritual vigor of their lives. He discovered in them mental powers equal to his own, while in lofty purpose they were vastly his superiors. For the first time in his life he felt something lacking in his own manhood. He saw he was living on a lower plane of life than the one upon which they were living.

One day he made the discovery that Paul Stanhope was interested in their lady companion to more than an ordinary degree, and at the same time observed that this discovery troubled him. Why should it? As he meditated upon this question, searching the depths of his heart, he felt that a love for the fair maiden had touched him also. He paced the deck for hours as the night passed, arguing with conscience what course he should pursue. Now he felt his weakness as never before, and the nobility of a life consecrated to Christ flashed upon him with such splendor as to cause every form of pleasure to sink into the surrounding darkness. At length he conquered his own soul and determined that, if Paul Stanhope loved the maiden and the maiden returned that love, he would not in any way put a stumbling-block in their path. They were consecrated to do Christ's work. They could do it better together than apart. He had no such motive; he sought only personal pleasure, and he could not ask this maiden to lower herself by stepping down to his plane. Therefore, with true manly courage, he fully gave her to his rival.

There were a number of English officers on the vessel returning to their stations in India, having enjoyed a furlough of a few months in their native land. As they sat on the quarter-deck in a group, they helped the time to pass rapidly by recounting their various adventures in India, the land of promise, financially and officially, to them. They seemed to be a merry group, and the dusky coolie servants attending them were kept busy bringing from the refrigerator bottles of claret and champagne. As they became noisy, uttering their jests in loud voice and singing fragments of camp songs, one of them, evidently ashamed of his companions, withdrew from them, and, seeing the Americans sitting by the port railing, came and sat with them. Captain James Grey was a man past middle age. His frame was stout and compact, his features regular but browned by continued exposure, and his hair and whiskers were cut in prevalent military style. His keen eyes flashed evidences of unusual intellectuality across his still handsome countenance.

In India he had won his first spurs as a soldier in the famous Sepoy rebellion. Since then he had been with Gordon in China, and latterly in Egypt. From Khartoum he had escaped, and had been allowed a period of rest in England. Now he was returning to India to take command of one of the prominent mountain fortresses. He was a man with a history, and was interesting to all who came into his presence.

As he came up to the Americans he pleasantly remarked: "Only a day or two and we will be in India; the most wonderful land under the sun. Did you know, Miss Thompson, that some people think that the Garden of Eden was located just south of India, on an island named Lamuria; an island which, like the wonderful Atlantis of the Atlantic, has sunk beneath the ocean?"

"I did not know that," she replied, "but I have heard that, if Eden was as beautiful as Ceylon, our first parents deserved all the punishment they got for not appreciating it as they should, and that we poor mortals living elsewhere can only realize our great loss by a visit to that lovely island, latterly known as Buddha's paradise."

"You seem glad to be so near India again," remarked Mr. Morgan.

"Indeed, I am glad," replied the captain. "I feel as if I were returning home. Ah, sir, when I first left India I little thought that I should ever yearn for it as home—but such it has become to me."

"When did you first come to India?" asked Mr. Stanhope.

"Just before the mutiny in 1857," replied the captain, "and my first experiences were in the midst of barbarities the most terrible ever known in warfare. Now every thing is changed. The fleeting years have left their marks, and, although India is a land where the people cling with wonderful tenacity to the customs of their ancestors, the great influx of foreigners is having a modifying and reconstructing effect in all parts of the land. You would never suppose, from seeing them, that a people could change so suddenly and so terribly as the Hindus did in that awful mutiny, but it is an evidence of the power of a man's religious prejudices over his reason and his natural tenderness of heart. When you offend a people's religious convictions you turn loose a nature as ferocious as a tiger's."

"I have read many accounts of that terrible time,"

said Miss Thompson, "and I have wept at the recital of the cruelties then perpetrated, but I have never heard an eye-witness tell of it. Would it be asking too much of you, captain, to tell us about it?"

With a gallant bow to the fair questioner, the soldier replied: "Nothing would be a trouble to me that would afford you pleasure, but I fear if I were to picture to you the scenes through which I have passed, your tears would flow afresh many times. But I will tell you something about India which may be a help to you in understanding the present state of society, and explain why it is so difficult for even the Gospel to reach these benighted people."

The captain then turned to his valet, and said:

"Dennis, bring some refreshments. Miss Thompson, will you have some claret?"

"No, I thank you," she replied, "I never drink wine. I belong to the Women's Christian Temperance Union."

"O!" he replied. "Wel', you are better off; wine-drinkers fare badly in the hot climates; but you will have some soda?"

"Yes," she replied, "I am quite fond of soda."

Dennis at once brought soda-water, and when they had emptied their glasses, removed them and disappeared.

CHAPTER III.

THE ORIGIN OF CASTE.

DENNIS O'SHANE, the valet of Captain Grey, was an Irishman of purest Celtic stock. Large in body, ruddy in countenance, hair of reddish hue, garrulous, impulsive, keen in wit, strong as a giant, yet tender as a woman, devoted to his master, and inclined to be pleasant to every body, he won the regard of every one while convulsing them with mirth.

Dennis was allowed great liberties because he had served his master faithfully for many years. In battle and in hospital he had saved his master's life. The captain, fully understanding him, was not disposed to resent his kindly familiarity.

The other servants on the vessel were unusually polite to Captain Grey. They were as reverential to him as if he were an exalted being. Dennis was the cause of this unusual respect, for, when not on duty, he had gathered them about him, and with his rich flow of adjectives had spoken to them of his master in an unlimited ascription of impossible achievements. It was more than likely that if any of them had disputed the truthfulness of these assertions, Dennis would have attempted to break the offender's head. The Americans were nearly convulsed with amusement one day to hear Dennis talking to an unsophisticated servant about his first trip away from home. With a very patronizing air, and with all the pomposity he could command, he said:

"Sure an' yez will be mightily plazed wid the grandeur of Indi', an' it is myself plainly remimbers the look of the natives a-bowin' in the dust when I walked the strate in the rear of Captain Grey. Ach! Patrick Muldoon! what would ye have said if ye had seen me thin, wid all me grandeur and gallantry, impressin' the people? But niver mind thot now. In India they revarse matters. The hills they cover with temples, but the people mostly go widout clothes, save for the paint on their foreheads. They walk about as soft like as cats, an' take great pride in exhibitin' the shaved crowns of their luxuriant heads. Whin ye see the wimen on the strate, sure an' they are all clothed entirely in red, save for the white shawl that wraps them from head to foot, an' whin they ride, instead of walkin', it is in a little cart drawn by small white cows, or else in a small room built on poles an' shut in by curtains, the same being carried on the shoulders of four half-naked men, an' all lookin' too poor to tempt even buzzards. But whin they see yez a-comin', the sight of yez so strikes them wid amazement that they git down on the ground, wid their faces in the dust, for very reverance of yer greatness, do ye see. Ye must know the people of India are astonishin' polite, an' to show proper appreciation yez must hold your head high up, as if it was all true; an' whin ye spake to them be sure an' spake rael grand like, so as to impress thim with your spache as well as with yer appearance."

As Dennis said this, he attempted to show the servant how to walk and speak. His effort was so successful that the Americans could no longer restrain their mirth, and Dennis learned that his audience was larger than he had supposed.

They told Captain Grey of his valet's humor, and the captain laughed with them. Then to destroy the absurdity of the scene, said:

"Dennis is comical, but he is also very intelligent. I will call him and ask him some questions, and you will see he is well posted on India."

In obedience to the call Dennis immediately came, when the captain put the following questions, which Dennis promptly answered:

"What is the shape of Hindustan?

"Somewhat like that of an elephant's ear, sir."

"What is the distance from east to west?"

"About 1,900 miles, sir."

"What is the distance from north to south?"

"Nearly 2,000 miles, sir."

"What is the area of the country in square miles?"

"1,577,698 square miles, sir."

"What is its population?"

"300,000,000, and growing rapidly all the time, sir."

"How many of these are Europeans?"

"Only one out of every 3,500, sir."

"Is it possible," said Miss Thompson, "that there are so few Europeans there? How, then, does the English government hold possession?"

"Ah" replied the captain, "this shows the courage and grit of the English soldier. It also shows why England fears the crafty schemes of Russia; but, to fully comprehend it, the whole structure of government in India must be considered. The Hindus lack the power of organization. The English glory in perfect organization."

"Dennis, tell us if India is a great country?"

"Yes, sir, it is great. It is of great antiquity, of great wealth, of great resources. It has great rivers, great plains, great jungles, and great mountains. It has forty mountain peaks each of which is over 20,000 feet high, and Mt. Everest, in Nepaul, 31,000 feet high, is the highest mountain in the world."

"Well, Dennis, you did not mention cities, are they not great?"

"No, sir; excepting Bombay, which is the second city for size in the British dominions, India has no great cities. It is a land of villages. It has 493,000 town and villages. About 50,000 of these have over 1,000 each in population. But what they lack in cities they make up in buildings. As Bishop Heber said, 'They built like Titans, and finished like jewelers.'"

"How about its population?"

"It is the most thickly populated country on the earth."

"How many languages are spoken in India?"

"Twenty, sir."

"What are the principal ones spoken?"

"Sanskrit, Pali, Persian, Arabic, and English."

"Why are these the principal ones?"

"Because they contain the religious and legal writings of the various people of India, sir."

"You are correct in your answers, and may now retire with thanks of us all," said the captain, and, with a salute, Dennis departed.

"Alas! in what ignorance we poor mortals repose," said Miss Thompson. "To learn that twenty different languages are spoken in India, and many of these subdivided in various dialects, and what will do in one part of the land will not do in another, is indeed appalling. To talk to a Parsee we must know Persian; to a Mohammendan, Arabic; to a Buddhist, Pali; to a Hindu, Sanskrit, and, in the coast towns, a smattering of all languages known among men. Yet the good people of America think a missionary is, or ought to be, able to preach the Gospel anywhere, to any people. Why, in the very nature of things, a person's work is restricted to a limited sphere."

Mr. Stanhope said: "I should imagine the study of philology would be exceedingly interesting in India. In fact, if I remember aright, it was the discovery of Sanskrit to the European scholars that started philology as a distinct science."

"Yes," replied the captain, "I believe that is so; and the story of the Sanskrit is very interesting. The Aryan invaders of ancient India did not come all at once, but in successive streams, each differing from the other, not only in great length of interval, but in dialects, customs, and civilization.

"They all had their traditions, mythical heroes, and religious hymns. But their trouble was not having a common language. Then their priests, the Brahmans, did a noble thing. They took the various Aryan dialects, molded them into one grand, harmonious language, and gave the world the 'Queen of Aryan languages,' the sacred Sanskrit.

"But the work of the priests was not appreciated by the people, and they never made it their common language. They clung to their dialects, called Prakrits. The priests, however, preserved the Sanskrit, and in it wrote their sacred books, the Vedas. The Sanskrit is an unchangeable language. The Prakrits have been affected by the speech of every race that has entered India. It is therefore an evidence of the wisdom of those ancient priests to have made a language in which to preserve inviolate forever the sacred thoughts of the Aryan people.

"The most famous of these Prakrits is the Pali, the sacred language of Ceylon, in which the doctrines of Sakyamuni, or Buddha, are written. And although for ten centuries the new faith tried to overthrow the old, the victory has rested with the faith preserved in the unchangeable Sanskrit."

"I am delighted to know this," said Miss Thompson, "and I shall pursue my studies in Sanskrit with greater zeal than ever. Now there is another thing I wish you would make plain to me, captain; and that is the system of caste, which seems to be the great hinderance to all missionary success in India."

"I think I can make it plain," replied the captain, "if I can get you to see some things as I see them. You must first of all realize that the people of India are like ourselves in nature. Their ways of thinking, reasoning, reflection, and expression are very much like our own. And the same general features in sociology observed among us are observed in India. The spirit of caste is every-where. In England it is quite prominent, making the nobility or aristocracy on one hand, and the working people or trades people on the other. In democratic America class distinctions are largely recognized, even in churches; and the masses say the churches are for the classes. Capital is arrayed against labor, not only in the workshop, but in society. The South, you know, said, This is a white man's government; making the color line the basis of caste. Whether it is culture, or ancestry, or position, or wealth, or color, the fact is the same, it is caste. In India it has been reduced to a system, with well-defined rules, and centuries of bondage have preserved it as we see it to-day. It has its bad side, but it also has its good side. In theory you will probably see only its bad side, in practice you may see its good side. If you were to suddenly break down the system of caste you would turn India into a hell. It can only safely be broken down by the substitution of something better. Christianity will do it, and will do it for the good of India. People visiting India observe that the immorality of the people is appalling. They can only know this where caste is broken down. The system of caste is the protection of the morals of India. It builds a hedge about the people. It guarantees their safety. Do you not see what utter demoralization of ideas of propriety, and what destruction of virtue, would ensue if this hedge were removed from society as it is at present constituted? But, pardon me; I did not mean to argue the question, for I hope Christianity will destroy caste every-where. If you are not wearied I will try to explain how caste has grown to be what it is."

"O, thank you! Do go on, I am not at all weary," said Miss Thompson. And the gentlemen adding their encouragements, the captain continued:

"In the study of races and the migrations of men

we naturally look to the dispersion from the tower of Babel as the beginning; but this mysterious fact presents itself—wherever the children of Noah went they found people already settled there, and these aborigines invariably had almond-shaped eyes. They were Mongolian in type, and to-day scholars are eagerly awaiting the translations of the ancient writings of China to explain who the Chinese are, and how they are related to these ancient peoples of similar ethnographical features.

"The most ancient people of India particularly resemble the lower races found to-day in Africa. They were diminutive in size, black in color, with thick lips, high cheek bones, and beardless.

"All our knowledge of them is from traces lingering among succeeding races. The first descent upon these aborigines was probably not long after the building of the tower of Babel, when two diverse races entered India from the north. One of them, having almond-shaped eyes, came from the northeast. They are known as Kolarian. The survivors of this ancient race are of the rudest sort; feeble in intellect, retaining the most degraded customs, almost entirely discarding the use of clothing, and absolutely without a literature. You probably have observed the laborers doing the most menial work on the vessel; they are Coolies of Guzerat and Bheels of Rajpootana, both remnants of this ancient Kolarian race. You will see thousands of them in

Bombay crowding the streets where the hardest work is done. From the north-west—a route to-day distinguished as being coveted by Russia—there came a race called Dravidian, allied to the Scythian hordes of Central Asia. The ancient poem of the Brahmans speaks of them as 'uncouth, savage, given to horrible rites, eaters of raw meat, cannibals, and being giants or apes in form.' The descendants of these Dravidians now dwell in that part of India south of the Vindhya Mountains. They are much more numerous than the Kolarians, and number about forty-six millions.

"The Telugus, a people pronounced by some travelers to be as fine-looking as any class of men in India, are of this race. You will probably remember that they have responded to the calls of the missionaries with astonishing ardor.

"In the period following these invasions the land became densely populated, but the social customs continued to be of the rudest description. At a later period, probably about the time the pyramids were being erected in Egypt, the races known as Aryan began to migrate from the high lands of Asia. One stream went westward. The Europeans and Americans have descended from these. Another stream came southward, and, following the track of the Dravidians, entered India. This was followed by other streams, or migrating hordes, pushing on, battling continually, putting their superior civilization against the barbarism of the inhabitants of the land; and sweeping out of their way the weaker ones, or leaving them stranded here and there, like islands, the Aryans seized the fertile plains along the great rivers and established in them their permanent homes.

"The Aryans had a priesthood, traditions, heroes, and songs for worship and war. Their priests invented Sanskrit, wrote the Vedas, and classified mankind.

"For centuries their relentless warfare continued. It was race battling against race, civilization against barbarism. It was the question of 'the survival of the fittest.' Well, all have survived, because the inflexible decree of the conquerors made it possible. The system of caste, to preserve the strong from the disintegrating influences of the weak, was established, and ever since has been tenaciously observed by all. The conquered knows his place. He is a pariah; his obsequiousness to-day is an evidence of the thoroughness with which those ancient Aryans did their work. Originally, therefore, caste was a protection against inferiority; to-day it is a protection against vice. But, like many other good things, it has done its work, and is becoming a thing of evil and needs to be superseded by something better."

At this moment the bell sounded for dinner and the conversation was suspended.

CHAPTER IV.

INDIA'S RECORD OF BLOOD.

As they drew nearer to Bombay the temperature became the more delightful, and the passengers remained at longer intervals on the deck. The weariness and lassitude which they suffered while on the Red Sea were now entirely overcome, and the spirit of music was awakened.

The piano and a number of violins, which several of the officers played very well, were brought into service to accompany the choruses in which the voices of passengers harmoniously blended.

The Americans were together most of the time, but Mr. Morgan displayed a degree of restlessness which he alone knew was caused by his efforts to prevent Miss Thompson from unconsciously binding his heart to her own.

He looked for the end of the voyage with gladness, as he would then be relieved by circumstances from his temptation. Seeing Captain Grey approaching the group made room for him, and requested information of the later history of India. He was not unwilling to grant this, but insisted that they all have some ice-cream to prepare them for comfortable listening. Then he said :

"I will first speak just a word about the ancient writings of the people of India.

"The ancient epics of the Hindus are histories of the solar and lunar dynasties.

"The Ramayana tells of the adventures of Rama, the hero of the solar race, who conquered Ceylon about the year 1200 B.C. The Mahabharata describes the wars of the Pandus and Kurus, of the lunar race, about 1400 or 1300 B.C.

"There have been invasions since that day. Darius, the great Persian king, conquered the northern part of India, and made it a satrapy, and it contributed its contingent toward the immense army Xerxes hurled against Greece.

"Alexander the Great invaded India and conquered Porus at Guzerat. He would have overrun the whole country, but his soldiers became alarmed at his continual advancing and, by refusing to follow, compelled him to return. The Greek historians considered India as being wonderfully civilized, with opulent cities, and the arts and sciences in a high state of cultivation.

"This was the golden period of Hindu supremacy. At this time caste was not so offensively supported, and their females were neither so restricted nor despised. The degradation of the females we will partly lay to the Mohammedan invasion.

"The next invasion was by the Persians, and fire-worship and Zoroastrianism found root in India's soil;

but to-day it is restricted to the Parsees of Bombay, a class of people particularly distinguished for their wealth, culture, business tact, and thorough integrity. They command the admiration of all who know them.

"About the year 1000 A. D. the Mohammedans with sword and spear forced the passes of the Himalayas and swept down upon the land, to root out all opposing religions, and in their stead plant the faith of Mohammed.

"The first of these were Afghans, who had been fire-worshipers but had been converted to Islamism. They delighted in plundering Hindu temples, robbing cities, and murdering all who came in their way. Mohammed of Ghazni, in 1001 A. D., laid the foundation of the Mohammedan power in India. His flag was black, and under its folds the land reeked in blood for five hundred years. War was their delight, and every new monarch signalized the beginning of his reign by the murder of all that he suspected might be dangerous to the peace of the throne.

"In 1526 Sultan Baber, the Tartar governor of Cabool, a descendant of Tamerlane, and the son of a Mongol woman, overthrew the Afghan rule at Pampat, and established in its place the Mogul Empire. This was also a Mohammedan power, and it lasted until the mutiny of 1857. This was the period when all Europe was dazzled with the wealth and splendor of the Mogul court.

"In 1497 Vasco de Gama, the Portugese navigator, came to India, and was received with great pomp by the rajah of Calicut. There followed many voyages by these most enterprising of mariners, and they had a splendid opportunity to establish themselves in power; but they sought to Christianize India by the methods of the Inquisition, and as a consequence they were almost annihilated. There was left upon the Hindu mind an utterly false and ineffaceable idea of Christianity. In 1594 the Dutch came. In 1616 the Danes. In 1668 the French, and, for a time, under Dupleix, they were brilliantly successful in southern India.

"In 1579 Thomas Stevens, an Englishman, published an account of his travels in India. As a result Queen Elizabeth incorporated by charter the British East India Company, giving them the control of all the trade between England and India. In 1600 the English entered India. The first blood shed between the English and the natives was in 1664, when Sigani, the famous Mahratta chieftain, attacked the town of Surat, and was driven back by the English.

"In the war between the French and the English for the supremacy in southern India Clive first won his laurels, but the natives of India did not feel the awful grip of England's iron hand until the tragedy of the Black Hole in Calcutta. The English factories were being established in Bengal, but they were not so important as those in Madras. In 1756 a new ruler ascended the throne of Bengal, Behar, and Orissa. He suddenly attacked the English. The women and children were sent to the ships, while a hundred and forty-six Europeans remained in Calcutta to treat with Nawab Surajah Dowlah. The angry nawab entered the city on a sultry evening in June, and crammed the entire number of Europeans in a dungeon eighteen feet square, having only two small breathing holes. In the morning all but twenty-three of the one hundred and forty-six were dead. They were suffocated by the heat and the poisoned air of the dungeon.

"At the time of this awful tragedy Clive was in Madras. He at once hastened to Bengal, and demanded complete satisfaction from the infamous murderer. The nawab armed his hosts to meet the English. He had 50,000 infantry, 18,000 cavalry, and an immense train of artillery. Clive had only 650 European infantry, 150 gunners, 2,100 Sepoys, 10 pieces of artillery, and a few Portuguese; but he determined on the battle, and on June 23, 1757, the battle of Plassey was fought. Clive was thoroughly victorious and India lay at his feet. The murdered Europeans were avenged.

"For a hundred years the English grew in power, and seemed to possess the confidence of the people. Rulers and people were alike respectful and kind. But in reality beneath this smooth surface there was being culminated the most terrible scheme to drive out the English and restore the power and splendor of their native princes.

"It seemed impossible that the Hindus and Mohammedans could ever unite in any cause, for they held each other in the most deadly hatred; but they entered into this conspiracy and with equal cruelty attempted the merciless extermination of the foreigners.

"The English offended the Moguls by abolishing the costly pageant of a dethroned monarch. They offended Nana Sahib, the leader of the Hindus, by refusing him the titles and annuities which the man who had adopted him as a son had held. Hence he became the most heartless conspirator of them all.

"He entertained in his palace with great apparent cordiality numbers of English officers, and seemed to be tenderly solicitous for their possession of every comfort; and at the same time he had doomed every one of them to a cruel death.

"The fakirs were the principal agents in carrying messages from the courts of the natives to one another, and the Thugs and murderers confined in all the prisons were promised liberation to engage in the work of massacre.

"The plot was to be ripe on the one hundredth anniversary of the battle of Plassey. They thought the power that rose on that day should fall on that day; and their astrologers had declared that if they did not beat the English on that day the British would hold

India forever. As the time approached, the Sepoy army held the forts, magazines, and treasuries of India. Every thing was in their hands. There were only forty-five thousand European troops in all India, and of these twenty-one thousand were in Madras and Bombay. Two thirds of the others were on the western frontier and in Burmah. The English officers had such confidence in their Sepoy, or native Brahman, troops, that they could not believe they would rebel. But the annexation of their home, Oudh, and the growth of missions, leading them to think their religion was about to be overthrown by force, excited them to highest frenzy. Falsehoods appealing to their prejudices were also freely circulated. The year before the mutiny the Enfield rifle was introduced into the Sepoy army, to take the place of the "Brown Bess" muskets they had been using. This rifle required a peculiar cartridge which was to be manufactured at the arsenal near Calcutta. The fakirs said these cartridges were greased with hog's lard and bullock's fat, and it was to destroy their religion. The Hindu has a wonderful reverence for the cow, and the Mohammedan an equal horror of the hog, so that this statement set them all wild with frenzy. The fakirs also asserted that the English had imported several cargoes of flour mixed with bones which had been ground fine, and one morsel of it would destroy the caste of any man; and that this flour had been covertly introduced and was then on sale in all the leading bazaars, but so well disguised that even the dealers could not detect it. Imagine the effect of such tales from their religious leaders! In February, 1857, took place that singular circulation of small unleavened cakes called "chupatties." Each recipient of two cakes was to make ten others and transmit them in couples to the constables of the nearest village, and they to others. This singular warning excited the whole country, and yet the English were utterly ignorant of any trouble. Before the set day came the mutiny was precipitated, and this saved the English cause in India.

"I will not distress you by depicting the scenes of fiendish cruelty that marked every step of this mutiny. Such cruelty has never been surpassed in human warfare. And, on the other hand, there have never been brighter exhibitions of courage and trustworthiness than were displayed by the soldiers of the English army. Many of the Sepoys, too, remained faithful, and the natives also who had become Christians were as true and brave as the best of Europeans. Terrible as was the conflict, the power of the English triumphed, the mutiny was suppressed, and the perpetual sovereignty of the land won for England.

"At present India is more prosperous than ever before. Railroads and broad thoroughfares are binding all parts of the country together. The true appeal of Christianity is being better understood, and the day may not be far distant when the elaborate temple and mosque worship will be a thing of the past."

"God grant it!" Paul Stanhope devoutly said.

The captain now withdrew, amidst the hearty thanks of the entire party. As he walked away Dennis whispered to Mr. Morgan, "Sure, sir, the captain himself was a great sufferer in that bloody time. His home an' all his loved ones were destroyed. An' it is his grief to this day."

Miss Thompson heard the remark and understood why the captain had refrained from giving harrowing details.

CHAPTER V.

BOMBAY.

AT an early hour on the following morning, while the rising sun was rapidly scattering the mists that hung low over the horizon, the passengers went on deck and crowded the bow of the ship, each one eager to be the first to catch sight of Bombay. At length the lookout, seated in his lofty perch in the rigging, called out, "Land ahead!" and in a few moments the passengers saw the beautiful city rising out of the waters before them, and those familiar with its towers called the names of the prominent objects as they rapidly appeared.

Bombay is built on the end of an island eight miles long and three wide. It connects with Salsetta, another island, and with the main-land by long viaducts. The harbor is unrivaled in the world for beauty, and furnishes a safe anchorage for vessels of all sizes.

Among the beautiful islands in the harbor is Elephanta, famous as the site of ancient templed caves, and the resort of all travelers to India. The mainland on the east side of the harbor is thickly fringed with luxuriant groves of stately palm-trees, amidst which are to be seen pagan temples of all styles, each one showing by its peculiar form whether it is the resort of Hindus, Parsees, Jainas, or Mohammedans. Back of the coast rise the Ghauts, or mountain ranges, the faces of which are diversified by terraces, spires, pointed peaks, and rounded summits. Upon some of these the ruins of old Mahratta castles glitter in the sunlight, constant reminders of the terrible battles by which the Hindus attempted to defend their land from the Mohammedan invaders.

The rock-bound, cup-shaped harbor, with its border of luxuriant foliage, forms a beautiful setting for the island city, a city second in size in the great British Empire, while in its variety of population it stands as the most wonderful in the world. Bombay was a part of the marriage dowry of Catharine, Princess of Portugal, which she brought to Charles II. in 1662. It received its name from Bamba Devi, a beautiful Hindu queen who lived before Alexander the Great visited India, and who was worshiped after her death, in one of the oldest Hindu temples on the island, as the Great Mother.

Bombay's wonderful harbor attracted the attention of the East India Company, and they made the town their capital. From that time until now it has rapidly and substantially grown.

Slowly the vessel drew up to the Mayagon Bunder; the passengers bade each other farewell, then climbed up the great granite steps to the quay. After entering the custom-house and attending to its demands, they passed out into the street, and were in India. As they entered the square the peculiar life of India at once burst upon them. Bare-legged Hindus, clothed in snowy-white garments, with immense turbans on their heads, humbly asked the privilege of taking the strangers to their destination. Their conveyances had oblong, box-shaped bodies, with latticed windows, set on wheels and drawn by small white oxen.

The streets were swarming with people. Everywhere it was like the front of a bee-hive in flower season.

White robed Brahmans, Buddhists, Jainas, Hindus, Chinese, Persians, Arabs, Africans, Indo-Portuguese, Indo-Britons, Jews, Arminians, Afghans, Caucasians, Parsees, Americans, French, Germans, Italians, English, soldiers, and policemen. The streets were almost lined with policemen, who never failed to touch their hats to the English or Americans as they passed by them.

But the great crowds of Asiatics, dark brown in color, were the most curious of all. The coolies, or common laborers, went about with only a strip of cloth covering their loins and immense turbans on their heads. House-servants wore a little more clothing. Low caste women, or women below caste, were in the crowds overdressed in the most gaudy colors, crimson, scarlet, yellow and blue being favorite colors.

There were also Hindu maidens with ear-rings,

nose-rings, bracelets, and huge silver anklets on their naked feet, with scant clothing and a profusion of ornaments, going their various ways. The men attempted to add to their attractive appearance by coloring their lips a brilliant red, and placing upon their foreheads stripes of coarse pigments, these being the symbols of their different castes. In every direction the streets were filled with crowds of these people, and the little ox carts were welcomed as friends in the hour of need.

At the door of the custom-house our friends parted. Miss Thompson was soon safely stowed in a roomy ox-cart, with instructions to the driver to land her safely at the mission schools in Byculla, one of the suburban places under the special patronage of several wealthy English ladies of high rank. Rev. Mr. Stanhope then entered a cart and was driven to the residence of a missionary, who was awaiting his arrival to introduce him to his future work in Benares.

Mr. Morgan was taken through the entire city to Watson's Hotel, one of the finest hotels in the world, and Captain Grey, with Dennis, proceeded to the English barracks on the promontory, where the English soldiers had the benefit of the most delightful breezes to be enjoyed in Bombay.

Miss Thompson was cordially welcomed at Byculla, and was made to feel at home by the kind attentions of those who had also left home and mother to do the Lord's work in India. One of the ladies, whose purse was always open to advance the missionary work, insisted on entertaining Miss Thompson in her own home at Colabah. This part of Bombay was on the lower part of the promontory, just below the soldiers' barracks. It was on a spot between two bays, and the site of many bright, airy bungalows, from whose broad, shady verandas the harbor, with its huge ocean steamers and thousands of small boats, could be seen on the one side, and the busy, throbbing life of the city on the other. Here, too, they could hear the music of the English bands, as every evening they saluted the going down of the sun by the rendition of national airs.

When her guest had rested sufficiently from the long journey the English lady sent for her carriage to take them through the bazaars of the city. The wealthy people of Bombay prided themselves on the elegance of their turn-outs, and even the drivers, with the spirit of Arabs, talked to their horses as to companions.

They directed the coachman to drive first through the markets of the Parsees. These were the most famous of all the merchants in Bombay. The markets were at least three miles long, and were in great blocks of lofty houses built in the prominent Oriental style, having wooden balconies and latticed windows projecting over the street, displaying elaborate carvings, and festooned with costly tapestries. These buildings were homes as well as markets. The merchants lived in the upper stories, while the ground floors were used as stores and the alcoves as shops in which native artisans made the articles sold. Here kinkaubs, or cloths of gold, were woven, and also mulmuls, or muslins, of such transparent texture as to be called "running waters."

In some of the shops half-naked men and women, with tools as rude and savage-looking as their own faces, sat making drinking-cups, boxes, and fans out of cocoa-nut shells; and tables, chairs, and other articles of furniture.

They seemed to be accustomed to the curiosity of foreigners, and did not mind the coming of visitors, but steadily continued at their labor.

After watching their peculiar way of working for some time, the ladies entered their carriage and drove to the Bhendee Bazaar. Here they saw the real mixed life of Bombay. The streets of the bazaar were densely crowded. Carriages of Europeans; draped carriages, drawn by milk-white bullocks, conveying Hindu or Parsee ladies closely veiled; native soldiers pressing through the crowd; native women, clothed in handsome dresses, going from stall to stall; coolies, with only a cincture around their loins, struggling along with immense burdens on their heads, some of them so hidden that only a pair of bare legs were seen under the bulky burden; Mohammedans wearing elaborate turbans stopping to converse with merchants who were seated cross-legged in their dens, wearing turbans and long-flowing robes, and smoking long hookas; beggars clamoring for assistance, cripples displaying their infirmities, vagabonds standing in the way, peddlers continuously yelling to attract attention, and dogs yelping as if trying to make the most noise of all, while in shady spots loungers lay sleeping, utterly indifferent to every thing. Out of this confusion they were glad to return to the cool verandas, where Jennie rested and regained strength to begin work on the morrow.

Mr. Morgan was delighted with Watson's Hotel. It was like home, for the managers carefully studied the tastes of their guests, and employed every means to gratify them. Numbers of servants moved about with silent tread. They seldom spoke, and with quick intuition anticipated the needs of those whom they served; hence the guests always found ready at hand just what they desired.

This faculty is one of the features of the Hindoo character.

At the time of Mr. Morgan's arrival the social season was at its height, and the pleasure-loving people spent every evening in elaborate social entertainments. His letters of introduction opened the way for a cordial reception by the people dwelling on Malabar Hill, and he was at once received into the social life of the *élite* of the city.

He had come to India for pleasure, and as he tasted of the amusements indulged in by the wealthy

A NAUTCH GIRL.

people of Bombay the opportunities for his gratification appeared to be boundless.

At one time during the voyage from Suez he came under the spell of Jennie Thompson's influence, and seriously thought of changing his plans and trying to be useful to his fellow-men. But the effort to break away from the spell of love for the pretty missionary led him to throw himself the more vigorously into lively associations, and he did not return to the more serious purposes of life. Their aims were so much higher than his own, their courage so much more profound, their zeal so much more fervent, that he hastily bade his friends farewell, and plunged into such pleasures as tended to hush the voice of conscience, and prevent its calling to him to give up the lower and seek the higher.

The entertainments given by the society people in Bombay were, he found, of a peculiar character. It was considered beneath the dignity of a lady to engage in sports of any kind. Although they were all ardent admirers of the dance, for a lady to have engaged in it would have been considered a most disgraceful act. The dancing was done by nautch girls, hired for the occasion out of establishments in which they were carefully trained in all the arts necessary to make their performances pleasing to the eyes and ears of their audiences. A nautchnee must have bright eyes, regular white teeth, long hair, and form and features of perfect symmetry. They were a class below caste, and mostly of unknown parentage, sacrificed to feed the licentiousness of men. Many of them were from Cutch, Cabool, Cashmere, and Rajpootana, having been taken from their homes when little children, and because of their beauty purchased to be trained for this kind of a life. Their beauty and culture often made them attractive to rajahs, or wealthy nabobs, who would pay as high as five thousand dollars for one to grace their harem. Admired although many of them were, for their beauty and skill, they were not happy. They were like lost waifs upon the sea of life, the better ones living in dread apprehension as they saw multitudes of their number going down beneath the waves of vice.

The last entertainment of the season that Morgan attended was given by a liberal Hindu gentleman who lived in a palace of great splendor on Malabar Hill. It was in honor of his daughter Dasee, whom Morgan considered the most attractive maiden he had met in Bombay. Refinement and luxury had surrounded her from her infancy. Morgan was honored with her friendship, and to him she confided the information that the entertainment would be made attractive by the performances of the most brilliant nautchnee in Bombay. The entertainment began with the usual brilliant cup-dance. At the opening Morgan's thoughts were absent from his surroundings. He was thinking of the pure, sweet face of the missionary.

A burst of applause caused him to look upon the stage, where he beheld a number of beautiful nautchnees keeping time to music, as they advanced in line. Standing apart from these girls, waiting her turn to perform, was one whose face was a perfect oval. The delicate olive complexion was purer and more transparent than that of her companions. Her eyes were large and brilliant, and her features were perfectly rounded. A slight tinge of pink touched her cheeks, and when she smiled her rows of perfect, brilliant teeth seemed to mark the climax of her marvelous beauty. She was clothed in the usual garb of a nautchnee, the contour of her symmetrical body showing through the drapery that encircled her form. When she sang, the audience was held spell-bound by her rich cadences, which was increased by the touching melancholy which at times swept across her face. Edward Morgan gazed upon her with utter surprise. Such a picture of grace and beauty he had never seen; not even in his dreams. When she danced, she seemed to be the personification of grace, and as, in closing her dance, she swept from the stage the people were wild with applause.

He wondered if she would appear again, and his thoughts turned to the stories he had heard of the strange lives many of these nautch girls lived. He asked himself, "Can vice be the delight of so beautiful a creature as that?"

CHAPTER VI.

THE NAUTCHNEE.

THE beautiful nautchnee displayed her highest charms in the delineation of scenes in the great Hindu epic, the Mahabharata.

This Sanskrit poem is the delight of all educated Hindus. It is to them what Homer's epics were to the Greeks, or Shakespeare is to the English; embodying their highest conceptions of poetic representation.

The greatest culture of the nautchnee was dedicated to the performance of these dramas, and the dressing of the various characters gave opportunity for the display of all their charms of feature and person.

Edward Morgan looked upon this Hindu amusement as a curious phase of Bombay social life. Suddenly, however, he was startled, for he again beheld the nautchnee who had so captivated him by her skill in dancing. She had entered to personate Damayanti, the Vedic beauty; "whose beauty disturbed the souls of gods and men." She wore on her head a crown of a pattern peculiar to the ancient days. Her hair was unbound, and in soft silken tresses hung down to her feet. She wore a gown, sleeveless, and open at the throat, exposing her arms, neck, and part of the breast. It was a fabric of the finest texture. It was ornamented by a complete hem of variegated silk, and fastened at the waist by a silk scarf. Over her entire figure was thrown a veil of such fine web-like texture that it seemed to be floating in the air about her like moats dancing in a sunbeam. As she entered into the spirit of the play her lovely features expressed all the phases of passion, sorrow, joy, and triumph which the drama called for, and when at length the play ended and she withdrew the audience for a moment seemed spell-bound by the marvelous beauty they had beheld. Edward Morgan's mind was in a tumult of passion. He recalled the fact that the beautiful creature who had displayed such marvelous grace and culture was not considered as worth a serious thought to the Hindu ladies of Bombay.

She was ostracized from the homes of the refined and noble, doomed for life to be only an entertaining machine. In his own land he had known men to lavish wealth and honor upon those whose genius enabled them to display attractions of person and mind far inferior to what he had just beheld. To his American ideas of equality the nautchnee was as noble as they, and in recognition of her powers he would lay his homage at her feet.

He could not associate such beauty and grace with loathsome lust. He knew she was not despised because of sins she had committed. It was only because she was the child of an inferior social caste, and the accident of birth forever condemned her to remain in this degraded position. He began to think of her as a pure white lily in the midst of a dark, mucky swamp, and, as the thought grew upon him, he determined to enter the noisome swamp, pluck the lily by the root from its bed and plant it in a garden of refinement and queenly graces, where it properly belonged. With his mind disturbed by conflicting emotions he went to his hotel, to recall the scenes through which he had passed, and to determine the best course to pursue to accomplish his purpose.

Nemorama had noticed the thrilling gaze of the American, and had felt her heart almost burst its bounds as she recognized in his eyes a passion she had never before observed in man.

For the first time in her life she felt the thrill of true appreciation, the touch of heart to heart, and she rose from the position of a machine to that of a gifted human being. From that moment she ceased to play for gold; she simply consecrated all her powers to that one appreciative listener. She knew she was surpassing herself, and astonishing all who beheld her, but the time had come; her hero was before her. A wild ambition seized her: it was to escape from the limitations of her life, and feed upon such food as was now given her. O, the delight of that hour! It ended all too soon.

When the curtain dropped she retired to her dressing-room and wept as she had never before in all her life. It was leaving the bright sunlight to sink into the gloom of darkness.

With her companions she hastened to her home; but in that one evening she had become a changed creature.

The nautchnee's home was in the most degraded part of the city. The house was surrounded by a high wall, within which was a court-yard ornamented by oleander and rose trees. In the midst of this yard was the building—divided into dormitories, training-rooms, and household apartments.

Nemorama hastened to her own room. It was small, and furnished with matting on the floor, a cot in which to sleep, a tier of boxes for her jewels and garments, some lotas, or drinking vessels, a few little mirrors, and some fancy ornaments which she had somewhere picked up. This was all. Divesting herself of jewels and robes she flung herself upon her cot, and, covering her face with her hands, struggled with the mysterious thoughts that surged through her soul.

She lay in this manner for some time, when she became conscious that some other person was in her room.

Rising quickly she saw standing near her a beautiful girl, only twelve years of age, watching her with curious, searching interest. She smiled as she saw the intruder, and, opening her arms, tenderly called her to come to her, and then, as she came, folded her in loving embrace.

"Ah, Saineh," she said, "is it you? Come to me, and let me rest my weary heart with your sweet love. You love me, Saineh, don't you? And don't you know I live on your love, my pretty darling?"

The child came to her, and at once seemed to be in complete sympathy with her, and the two fondled each other with such caresses as only the purest affection could inspire.

Five years before Saineh had been brought to this establishment. She was a little maid from the vale of Cashmere, and as beautiful as the morning's light. Her father, displeased with her being a daughter, despising girls as worthless, loving money for the gratification of his desires, sold his pretty child to the owner of this nautchnee establishment, and thus she came to be a companion to many others suffering a similar misfortune. When Nemorama saw her, she at once adopted her as her *protégée*, and for five years Saineh had been the delight of her life.

The child was a true Hindu. With a loving and confiding nature, she was always ready to lavish expressions of love upon her older and stronger friend. Her devotion partook of the nature of sympathetic absorption. She watched Nemorama's growing powers, and with strong imitative faculties followed her. Little by little she too was becoming expert, and, for a child, was already famous. The sweet tendencies of her soul shielded her from evil, and the wrath of Nemorama's stronger nature would have been freely vented upon any one who should attempt to harm her darling.

These nautchnees, cast out by their own parents and ostracized by society, owed their skill and grace to their severe training, and they felt the more completely their dependence upon their training establishment. It was their home, their arena of hope, and the place of rest; and the pure, service-loving Hindu hearts looked with dismay at the great outside world, and labored to amuse it only as machines. On nearly all these faces lingered an expression of sadness, of lonesomeness, which only departed under strongest excitement.

The following morning the nautchnees gathered in their training-room for their daily training. There were not less than a hundred of them in the room, and all were pretty—some of them wondrously beautiful. The room was furnished as a gymnasium, with rings, ropes, bars, and swings, to develop every muscle of the human body. Here they were trained for all kinds of dances and in gymnastic evolutions. All over the light bamboo trellis-work the ropes were swinging with the active girls seeking to be perfect in their performances.

Saineh was in great glee as she swung high up in the air, revolving in the swing and stretching out to its full length her supple body, showing such grace of motion as to awaken the admiration of even her trainers.

Suddenly there was a shriek, a body fell rapidly to the floor, and Nemorama rushed to the heap of flesh to find that it was her beloved Saineh. One rope of the swing had become detached, and the girl fell helpless. The blood flowed from her nose and mouth and she seemed to be dead. Nemorama carried her to her own cot and, tenderly washing away the blood, sobbed and moaned over her darling. Soon the little eyelids quivered, the breast heaved, and a moan came from her lips. Nemorama piteously called to her to waken and speak once more. The eyes opened and the little face smiled in response to the ardent pleadings, then she groaned with pain.

What could be done for the little sufferer? The attendants soon saw that the little girl must die, and her faithful friend was filled with deepest anguish. Seeing their distress Saineh guessed their thoughts, and asked them what would become of her when she died. The prospect of death filled the child with terror. It was an awful leap into the dark, a darkness filled with most terrible monsters, and no one could save her from her terrible fate. She clung impulsively to Nemorama, but she could only sing softly to her and try to divert her mind from the contemplation of death. The child had learned only of the endless succession of reptile or animal lives she would be compelled to live in the awful future. She was afraid of toads and snakes and worms, and the idea of being transformed into one of them made her suffering body quiver with fright; and, with her mind fastening upon the only ideas of death she had ever heard, she soon sunk into a high fever.

Nemorama was tenderly watching over her when a strange footstep was heard. The door of her room opened, and there entered a young woman whose face and dress at once indicated an American. With a pleasant smile she said, "I heard of the dreadful accident to one of your number, and came to see if I could help her. I am a physician, and understand how to set broken bones and subdue fevers." Then, coming to the cot, she gazed intently into the face of the child and tenderly touched her wrist.

Nemorama knew something of the skill of these American lady physicians and that they were highly esteemed by the high caste in Bombay, and she watched the visitor's expression to see if there could be hope for her darling. But the smile faded from the visitor's face as a look of deep pity stole into her features, and with true pathos she murmured, "Poor little maiden! How quickly such beauty fades!"

Nemorama understood the expression of the visitor's face, and, knowing these Americans were also teachers of religion, she fastened her anxious gaze upon her face and asked abruptly, "Where will Saineh go when she dies? Will she become a toad, or a snake?"

The visitor looked into the large, hungry eyes of her questioner, and said, "Did you ever hear of Jesus?" Nemorama slowly shook her head as she replied, "No, I never heard the name."

At that moment Saineh awoke, free from pain and curious to hear the words of the strange lady. Taking her hand, and gently stroking it, with tender tones full of pity and love the visitor told the story of Jesus.

She told of the glory he had with the Father; how he came to save men; how he sought out the poor and outcast; how he won the victory over death, on the cross; how he went into heaven to prepare the heavenly mansions; how he saves and glorifies all who trust in him. Then she pictured the glory of the redeemed ones in heaven, forever with the Lord. As she told this sweet story tears of joy flowed down the cheeks of her listeners, and Saineh in rapture said, "Now I am ready to die. O, I want to see the good Jesus. I know he will love me, for I shall love him with my heart. O, I am so glad you have told me of Jesus. It is all light now." Then she partly rose from the cot, her eyes grew large with a wondrous expression, a smile lit up her features, she said, "Why, there he is now! He is calling me. He calls, 'Saineh, Saineh, come to me, child.' His eyes are full of love to me. Yes, I am coming."

She tried to rise—to spring forward. Nemorama caught her in her arms, the blood gushed from her mouth, and when they laid her back on the cot they saw that she was dead.

The missionary physician departed, to tell the story of a Hindu soul saved and received into heaven by the Master. Nemorama with calm submission followed the body to the burning pyre, but comforted; for the chains of heathenism had been shattered, and she was walking with a new realization of life.

CHAPTER VII.

THE NAUTCHNEE'S HOME.

NEMORAMA returned to her home feeling that the tenderest chords of her heart had been sadly rent. No sooner had she found some one of kindred spirit than that one was taken from her. She felt utterly lonely and forsaken, without a single ray of light on her pathway.

As she thought of the friendship in the past, she wondered if Saineh and she were of the same race and caste. They had been like sisters. Both loved the same things, both had the same sad longings unfulfilled, and yet Saineh was of a gentler nature. She was frank, forgiving, and generally happy, while in Nemorama's heart there was constant tumult, dissatisfaction, and rebellion against the life she was compelled to lead. She had laid aside her robes, and was cherishing these sad thoughts, when a messenger came requesting that she put on her brightest jewels and appear in the audience-chamber. She obeyed almost mechanically. She knew from the manner of the summons that a stranger had come to examine her qualifications for some kind of an engagement, and she was not supposed to be sensitive in regard to the indelicacy of his scrutiny.

No time was allowed her to mourn the loss of her dearest friend. One day at the death-bed of all she held dear on earth, the next day dancing with gayest attire to please a fickle public. As she entered the audience-room she saw a handsome, brilliantly dressed Mohammedan talking with Bap, the master of their establishment.

With a single glance she measured the stranger, then, casting her gaze upon the floor, awaited her master's commands. Bap, the master of the Nautchnee home, was a keen, shrewd business man. For many years he had run this establishment, and had become rich through his good bargains. He bought only handsome girls, and took good care of them. In his way he was a father to them, and the only father many of them ever knew. He exercised supreme command over them because they knew he held in his hands the question of their happiness or misery, their life or death, and disobedience to him would receive an awful retribution. His word was law; they had no will beyond his word. He said to them "Do!" and they had no choice but to respond to his bidding. They were in his hands as tools to play with, and he always played for money.

As Nemorama stood in silence, the stranger carefully observed her for a few moments, then in the boldest manner came forward to examine her. He unrolled her luxuriant hair, felt the firmness of her arms, looked at her teeth, noticed the symmetry of her figure, and then engaged in low tones in conversation with the master. He had seen Nemorama at the same performance in which Edward Morgan had beheld her, and already knew the grace of her motions, and the power and sweetness of her voice.

At length the men finished their conversation, and the stranger coming near her said: "Most beautiful of women, with astonishment and rapture I, an unworthy dewan, have beheld your charms. Your excellence is so great that the multitudes are not worthy to gaze upon you. As a brilliant diamond you should be reserved for the crown of royalty alone. I have, therefore, come to convey you to the palace of my princely master, the rajah of the north-west, to illuminate his harem with a brilliancy unapproachable in any other part of the world. And may your power exceed that of Noor Mahal, who was the most beautiful of women."

The dewan then bowed before her, and stood with folded arms to receive her reply. Nemorama was startled by this fulsome speech, and, with an expression of consternation on her face, looked appealingly to Bap for explanation.

In response he said: "You are no more my child; you are the property of this man's master. You are to become a great princess if you please him; if you do not you will be hidden in darkness forever. You have been a good girl, and I am sorry to part with you, but such is life. Go! and may you be happy."

Then she realized it all.

She was sold to enter the harem of a stranger, to give her life to one whom she had never seen. She had no choice, no voice in the matter. A certain sum of money was considered an equivalent for her. The attachments of her soul, the desires of her heart, were of no account.

She did not want to go. If she went she would be the plaything of a Mohammedan, and she hated the oppressors of her people. She would be shut up in a harem, and she delighted in the applause of the people. She would never see the American again, and the hopes of her life would be blasted.

The tears began to flow down her cheeks, and as she covered her face with her hands her body shook with convulsive weeping.

Bap was moved by her distress, and was gratified at her reluctance to leave his home. It was an indorsement before the stranger of his kindness to his girls.

He tried to soothe her by saying: "Farishta, the dewan will take good care of you. You will be surrounded with every luxury and become a great lady, and then you will willingly forget the plainness, the poverty and severity of a nautchnee's life."

Nemorama sadly withdrew to her little room. Her companions gathered about her, and while some wept at her departure, others congratulated her on the good fortune that had come to her. She distributed among them her robes, jewels, and ornaments as keepsakes; for the dewan had provided new and more costly things for her. Taking only the little lota which had belonged to Saineh, she bade them farewell, allowed the dewan to veil her features, "to be seen henceforth only by the rajah," as he said, entered the palanquin provided for her, and at once began the journey to the rajah's kingdom in the north-west.

Bap would have felt great sorrow at her departure were it not for the ten thousand rupees he had received as her price. When he looked at these his sorrow melted and disappeared. He was still considering how to invest them to the greatest advantage, when a servant knocked at the door and announced the approach of a stranger to see his master.

As the stranger entered, the host bowed low, for he recognized before him the handsome American in whose honor several *fêtes* had lately been given in which his nautchnees had been employed.

Edward Morgan was laboring under suppressed excitement which he only partially concealed. His whole manhood had been aroused, and, with American enthusiasm, he was seeking to do the work that seemed to lie near his hand. After the entertainment in which he had been so strangely attracted by the Nautchnee he had been unable to sleep, for his mind was excited upon the probable life of the gifted girl.

In the morning a coolie came to him and informed him that a "holy man" was waiting to see him. Following the direction indicated by the coolie, he entered a grove near the hotel and there saw a fakir sitting upon the ground awaiting his coming. The fakir was almost naked. His hair had never been cut since the time he entered on his "holy" life, and was now longer than his body. It was wound around his head in a rope-like coil, and fastened with a wooden pin. His breast was daubed with a thick coating of paint and ashes. His arms and legs were bare, and seemed to be only skin and bone. His finger and toe nails were of enormous length. His eyes had a wild glitter that seemed to penetrate the soul of the person he gazed upon. Around his neck were strings of beads, and in one hand he held a stout club, his only defense when traveling in the jungle.

He seemed to be pleased with the promptness of the American's coming, and, re-arresting his attention, related the following narrative:

"At the time of the mutiny in 1857 there lived in the province of Oudh a Brahman of highest caste. The Brahman was the happy husband of a wife who had borne him three sons and a daughter, the daughter being only nine years of age. The father was about to give his daughter in marriage to a Brahman of the same caste when the approaching mutiny induced him to delay until the English, whom he hated, should be driven out of their land. As he expected this to be accomplished in a few months there would be no disgrace in his daughter remaining unmarried for that length of time.

"But the Brahman's sons were slain in the mutiny, and he was blown to pieces from the mouth of a cannon—the greatest dishonor that could have overcome him; for it prevented his soul from having a happy transmigration and left it to a disembodied wandering condition in the other world. The sad fate of the Brahman caused his wife to die broken-hearted, and the little girl fell into the hands of an English officer whose family had been put to death in one of the terrible massacres of that time. The officer with great kindness protected the child, and, when she had become of suitable age, charmed by her beauty, made her his wife. They seemed to be very happy together. He loved her, and she gave him all the faithful attentions a Hindu was able to give. Their happiness was increased by the birth of a daughter, and the child promised to be as beautiful as the mother.

"When the child was just getting old enough to lisp its mother's name the officer was sent on a mission to a neighboring city. When he returned his wife was dead, his house closed, his servants scattered, and, notwithstanding the most diligent search was made, no trace of his child could be discovered.

"The Hindu relatives of the woman had put her to death because she turned from her caste to marry the foreigner, and they sold the child to a Soudanese merchant, who disposed of it to some dealer in girls for nautchnees."

After a few moments of silence the strange fakir continued:

"Although the Hindu woman had married the officer she was always charitable to the fakirs, and many times she fed me with choice food, and I loved to see her happy face as she caressed her little babe.

"When the officer found he could glean no tidings of his child he went away and never returned. When the story was told to me of the sad desolation of his household, for the charity the mother had shown me I determined to find the child and watch over it.

"I at once began the search. I was fortunate in getting on the trail. I followed the child through many provinces until it came to this great city. I watched the place it entered and the progress it made. I watched that child until yesterday.

"She is now as beautiful as was her mother, but fairer in face and more supple in body. She knows not the purity of her birth; she knows not that any one has kept watch over her, although I have never lost sight of her. But, no matter; I am rewarded in knowing I have accomplished a good deed. My course is almost run. I have been waiting a long time for you to appear. I beheld you in my visions and knew you would come, so that I might commit her to your care. Last night you saw her. She is the beautiful nautchnee Nemorama. While watching your countenance I saw you look toward her. I know what that kind of a look means. It corroborates my visions. She is now in danger, and your work as her protector must begin. Go seek her. Defend her. If her father still lives find him, and restore his child to his aching heart and receive his priceless blessing and minè. Farewell!"

Suddenly the fakir disappeared. Recovering from his astonishment Morgan looked for him, but he had gone as silently as the falling of a leaf.

Morgan recalled his studies in esoteric Buddhism, and he felt the thrill of a mission committed to him from the unseen world. With solemn determination to succeed he accepted the obligation, and with American vigor so pressed his search that within an hour he stood at the gates of the nautchnee's home. In response to his inquiry for the fair Nemorama the master informed him that she had just been purchased by the dewan of a great rajah, and was already on the way to his dominions. In reply to his question, "Did she go by her own choice, and gladly?" the master said: "Nautchnees have no will, no choice; they are property; they are to provide amusement for the people, and to gratify the whims of those who have money to pay for them. The rajah had heard of her beauty and sent money to buy her, and she was sent to him. He might clothe her with elegant robes and cover her with jewels if pleased with her, or he might cast her aside for some other one that suited his fancy. As a creature to furnish men amusement this was her risk. As to her soul, she was below caste; that was all."

Morgan left the place with a troubled heart; his reflections were very bitter. Was this the price paid for the pleasure afforded the wealthy people on Malabar Hill? Could he, an American, knowing and believing in the Declaration of Independence, as written by Jefferson, consent to enjoy pleasure obtained from such a system and built upon the ruin of such creatures? No! his soul revolted at the thought. He returned to his hotel to study the route to the north-west most likely to be taken by the dewan, and to plan how he might intercept them and communicate with the maiden.

Before his plans were formed he received letters calling him to immediately prepare for a grand tiger hunt in the north of India, and to start without delay for the scene of action. As this was in the same direction the maiden was going, he returned word to Captain Grey that he would be on hand according to appointment.

CHAPTER VIII.

THE MOTHER'S SORROW.

CAPTAIN GREY assumed the responsibility of collecting the hunting outfit for the party, and this particularly pleased Dennis; for it gave him the opportunity of showing the bare-legged, white-robed Hindus how majestically he could give orders—"jist loike the ginerals to their armies."

As several days would elapse before all could be ready Morgan concluded to stop on the way and see some of the cities of historic renown, and search for a clue to the journeyings of Nemorama.

The railroad went direct from Bombay to Allahabad on the Ganges, where it joined the railroad from Delhi to Calcutta.

Morgan knew that the dewan would not travel by railroad, but by the time-honored and seclusive palanquins.

Railroads were an innovation in India, and no high caste person would patronize them at first. Time alone would destroy their prejudices. In 1853 there were only twenty and a half miles of railroad in India. In 1887, there were thirteen thousand three hundred and eighty-six miles. The high caste Brahmans saw this development of European ideas with consternation, and to them the railroad was an institution of evil; hence they would not under any circumstances patronize it. From Allahabad Morgan went to Agra, and there remained for a few days awaiting the summons from Captain Grey.

He remembered that Miss Thompson had located in Agra, and, curious as to what success she had with the women of India in their zenanas, determined to call upon her. The zenana is to the Hindu home what the harem is to the Mohammedan home, that is, the part exclusively devoted to the women. He had an excellent excuse for visiting Miss Thompson, as there had been committed to his care several cordial messages to her from her friends in Bombay who knew that he would only too willingly deliver them. He also bore a message from Dasee, the cultured Hindu maiden living on Malabar Hill, who was deeply interested in the elevation of her sex in their zenana life. She looked upon all that were engaged in the good work as sisters.

Mr. Morgan found Miss Thompson happy in her work, and the doors of the lower castes were being gradually opened to her.

She found it to be exceedingly difficult to gain entrance to the houses of the high caste Hindus. They were excessively scrupulous in every religious observance, looking upon disrespect to husbands with horror, and avoiding with the greatest care every thing that might defile them. They would endure all manner of suffering rather than be touched by a man not of their own household, or by any person of lower caste.

The strength of their prejudices was seen in an incident related to Miss Thompson. Several Hindu ladies of high caste were traveling on camels along the highway, when the girth of one of the saddles became loosened, and the lady, partially fast to the saddle, was thrown under the awkward beast. An English gentleman, seeing the accident, rushed to her rescue. But the ladies begged him not to pollute her by his touch. He pleaded to save her, which he could easily do by lifting her out of the saddle, but she forbade him to do so, preferring to die rather than be saved in that way. The camel became unmanageable, and the woman was trampled to death. Her devotion to caste rules received the hearty approbation of her companions, and her memory was blessed as a martyr to purity and devotion.

Sometimes, however, Miss Thompson was sent for by those in great suffering, and as the fame of her skill spread the calls became more frequent. She was careful not to touch her patients unnecessarily, and instead of giving them her medicines informed them of the remedies to be obtained by people of their own caste.

By her attractive manner she gradually became a favorite in the zenanas, where her conversations were enjoyed as something new and refreshing. Then as she read to them from the Bible she awakened their astonishment at her learning, for most of the high caste women were utterly ignorant of books, and were afraid that some misfortune would come upon their homes if they were found with books in their hands.

She told Mr. Morgan that at times she suffered intensely from sympathy for the deluded people, who so constantly violated the plainest requirements of nature, and suffered the inevitable consequences, in order to maintain the rules of caste.

One day a little girl came to the missionary asking her to come and see her sick mother. Miss Thompson was surprised at the intelligence of the child, as she displayed in all her movements a winning simplicity and affectionate dependence in strong contrast with the self-assertion and overbearing manners of the boys. She at once went with the little messenger. After walking half an hour they came to the open fields in front of a poor woman's cottage. The dwellings of the Hindus vary, in size and accommodations, according to the wealth of their owners; this was one of the poorest, containing but one room.

The cottage faced the east, with entrance a little to one side of the middle of the front wall. Once a week every Hindu woman smeared her room and the yard of her dwelling with a solution of cow ordure. When this was done she ornamented the front of the door with the form of a lotus flower made out of a solution of lime or chalk. The lotus was chosen because emblematical of the name of God; too pure to be uttered, but supposed to bestow a magical charm on the dwelling upon which it is inscribed.

A single glance revealed to the missionary that all the requirements of Hindu law were faithfully observed about this cottage. Through the open doorway the missionary saw the sick woman reclining upon a mat. By her side a healthy little babe was sleeping. On the floor, close by, another child was playing. The children were girls.

The woman was still beautiful, although sorrow had sadly marked her features. As she saw her visitor a bright smile illuminated her countenance, and she thanked her for coming so soon.

The missionary sat by her side and wept in tender compassion for her as she listened to the story of her life. Yet her story was a common one; how common only the mothers of girls in India know.

She said, "When but a child I was married to one of the noblest of high caste youths just after he had received the investiture of the sacred thread, signifying his entrance into all the duties and privileges of the caste preserved by his family from the most ancient times. He was a youth of great spirit, and seemed to be proud of his little wife; calling me his 'beautiful blessing.'

"When his relatives sought a wife for him they required of her certain characteristics. They said I possessed all of them. They said of me: 'She is free from all defects, is of a winsome and upright nature, has a soft and melodious voice, her name is pleasing to the ear, her motions are graceful, her features are regular, her eyes are strong and bright, her muscles are well developed, her teeth are perfect, her hair is rich and glossy, and she is very healthy.' The astrologers gave me a good recommendation, such as, 'she will be the mother of many sons, and will not outlive her husband;' hence great happiness was looked for in our marriage.

"From the time of the marriage until I was fully developed in physical powers I was trained by my husband's mother to prepare every kind of food suitable for a high caste Hindu to eat, and was thoroughly instructed how to keep his home. Then I was given to him, and I began to serve him.

"Like all Hindus he was very desirous to behold the face of a son, and for this earnestly besought the favor of the gods. A short time after we began to live together I visited the temple of Lakshina, attended by a neighbor who was the mother of several sons. I took a cake made of rice, sugar, and ghee or clarified butter; also a fresh cocoa-nut. I fervently offered my prayers before the shrine; then both of us spent some time in meditation on the glorious progeny of gods and heroes, after which my companion broke the cocoa-nut and poured out the liquid as an offering to the goddess. We returned home, and, with my husband's household, ate the rest of the cocoa-nut and the cake. When I knew that I would become a mother I went again to the temple, accompanied by the same friend, also by my father and husband.

"This time I was clothed in robes of spotless white which entirely covered me. Several Brahman priests officiated for us. We took oil, lighted tapers, and flowers. One of the priests took the oil, poured it on a lighted lamp, waved it over his head and uttered the prayer: 'O thou who art light, thou art also life and seed. Accept our sacrifice, and make the new life thou hast created in secret visible in beauty and strength and power of intellect.' After this we gave many valuable presents. As we returned home the priest made me very happy by saying, 'Mayest thou have eight sons, and may thy husband survive thee.'

"My husband repeated to me this law of Manu; 'Through a son a man conquers the world, through a son's son he obtains immortality, but through his son's grandson he gains the world of the sun.' My husband's father and grandfather were still living, and if I possessed a son their joy would be great through the blessings it would assure them.

"At length the greatest day of a Hindu woman's life came to me—the day of motherhood. The woman who accompanied me to the temple, the priest who had blessed me, and the astrologer, to cast the horoscope for my child, were in the room praying. When all was ready the attendants waved fire over my child, and put on its lips a drop of honey and butter out of a golden spoon. Then my husband came and looked into the face of his child; at the same time he took a piece of gold in his hand, anointed the child's forehead with clarified butter which had been first presented to Brahma, and then offered sacrifice to Brahma.

"He then bound a string of nine cotton threads with five blades of durba grass around the baby's wrist. The durba grass signified that the life should be made more perfect by the five daily sacraments.

"The astrologer then cast the horoscope for the child, which was written down and given into the keeping of the father.

"O, think of my grief and pain, in that moment of awful weakness, to hear my husband utter loud imprecations, and manifest tokens of extreme disappointment and anger. Alas! the child was a daughter. He angrily repeated to me the words of the law: 'There is no place in heaven for a man who is destitute of male offspring.' In that moment, when I needed the most tender care, every one turned from me with aversion.

"In front of the house many neighbors and friends had come to congratulate my husband. Musicians were there to make melody, and confectioners to scatter sweetmeats among the people. But my husband went to the door and announced in tones of contempt, 'Nothing has been born!' Then he retired to his room. The people returned to their homes. No sweetmeats were scattered, no music given, no joy manifested. It was only a girl, and in their estimation a girl was equivalent to nothing. But I could not help loving my little babe, and she grew strong and happy, notwithstanding the frowns and taunts of the older people.

"Two years later I was again about to become a mother. We offered more valuable presents in the temple. I purchased rosaries used by women who had borne many sons, and drank teas made of roots and herbs celebrated for their virtues. My devotions were assiduously given to trees and to those deities who bestowed sons. My husband declared that he would take away my ornaments and make me the family drudge if I did not give him a son. But alas! I again gave him another daughter. His people now uttered loud and severe complaints against me, and, incensed by their complaints, he became very angry. His grandfather was nearing the fulfillment of the time allotted to man, and he became an object of special pity because of my failure to give him honor in the other world. His father wept at the thought of his losses, and my husband became an object of pity to his companions. My husband declared that two calamities had come upon him, and that if it was so again I should be his wife no more. This threat filled me with horror. The third time I became a mother. But O, sorrow! a daughter was again placed in my arms. Then my husband cast me out and married another; for the law allowed him to do this. The awful severity of this punishment no one can know but those whose lives are bound up with their husbands. I loved my husband with all my soul, and I love him to-day as fervently as ever. I had always lived in luxury. My husband was very wealthy, and I was clothed with fine raiment and decked with costly jewels, and had many servants to do my bidding. To show his extreme displeasure he stripped me of all my ornaments and placed me in this bare and comfortless cottage. Here in poverty I must spend the remaining years of my life and never see his face again. My daughters are my comfort, and they bring smiles that drive away the tears. They are so loving, winning, and beautiful that, if I had my choice, I believe I would rather live just as I am with them than in luxury without them.

"When I was placed here every one commended my husband for his act of separation. They accused me of having committed some terrible crime in a previous life—of having poisoned a husband, or done some other awful deed—and now they avoid me and call me accursed. O lady, the people say you are wise and good, and that you teach a religion that comforts the sorrowing. Tell me, what can I do? Is it such a curse to bear daughters?"

Miss Thompson waited until the woman became calm, then told her of her own mother's household in distant America; her mother a widow and all her children daughters. Upon them no scorn was cast, no unusual burdens heaped, for the religion of Jesus taught them that girls were the equals of boys before the Lord, and daughters in America were loved and honored alike with the sons. The feeling of inferiority the daughters in India possessed was a degrading prejudice, offensive to the teachings and the will of the true God. Then she told the story of Jesus, God's Son, sent to save the world from its sin and the horrible darkness of its prejudices. The story of Jesus proved a balm to the wounded heart, and the poor woman eagerly received every word. When at length Miss Thompson departed the woman begged her to come again, and tell her more of the words of life.

When Miss Thompson arrived at the mission house she found Mr. Morgan awaiting her coming to take her on a visit to the Taj Mahal.

CHAPTER IX.

THE MOST BEAUTIFUL BUILDING IN THE WORLD.

THREE miles from Agra, in the midst of a spacious garden, stands the Taj Mahal; without doubt the most beautiful building in the world. A trip to India is not complete without a visit to this famous shrine. Morgan was exceedingly anxious to see it, and the delight of the visit would be increased by the responsive appreciation of so cultured an observer as Miss Thompson for his companion. He was thrilled with the thought that on this occasion she would be to him the personification of American taste, and together it would be America bowing before the memorial of Mohammedan love.

Mounting their palanquins, they were quickly conveyed to the gate by the fleet-footed coolie bearers, where they alighted, and, dismissing the coolies, leisurely walked about the grounds. They had many things to talk about, and, surrounded by the trees, flowers, and fountains of the garden, they spoke of America, the voyage, their companions, their purposes, and the wonderful building before them. A guide-book told them that it was designed by a Frenchman and built by the Mogul emperor Shah Jehan in honor of his beloved wife, Moomtaj-i-Mahal.

As they sat looking at its glistening white walls Miss Thompson said: "What strange contrasts this building suggests! Designed by a Frenchman, built by a Mohammedan, the peerless pride of a Hindu land, built in honor of a woman where women are despised. She was a ruler where her sex are enslaved. She died giving birth to a daughter; a fact of great repugnance to the dominant sex. While she ruled the kingdom her husband spent his time in revelry with drunken companions, and yet after her death he lavished the wealth of his kingdom in the magnificent attempt to honor her name. She only knew Christianity as it was taught by the Roman Catholics, and she hated it with all the ardor of her strong nature. On the end of the tomb facing the entrance there is inscribed, amid the flowers and jewels, a prohibition and a prayer against the followers of Christ, calling them by the contemptuous word 'kafirs.' The prayer reads, 'Defend us from the tribe of kafirs.' The emperor's orders were that none but men of Mohammedan faith were to be permitted within these precincts or to draw near her tomb, and express care was to be observed that no Christian foot approached it; yet to-day it is the Christian nation that protects the tomb, that honors the spirit of the emperor's ardent devotion, that holds woman in her true, loving, exalted station, and makes this tomb a temple for all mankind to visit as a memorial of the true and just honor granted one woman in India."

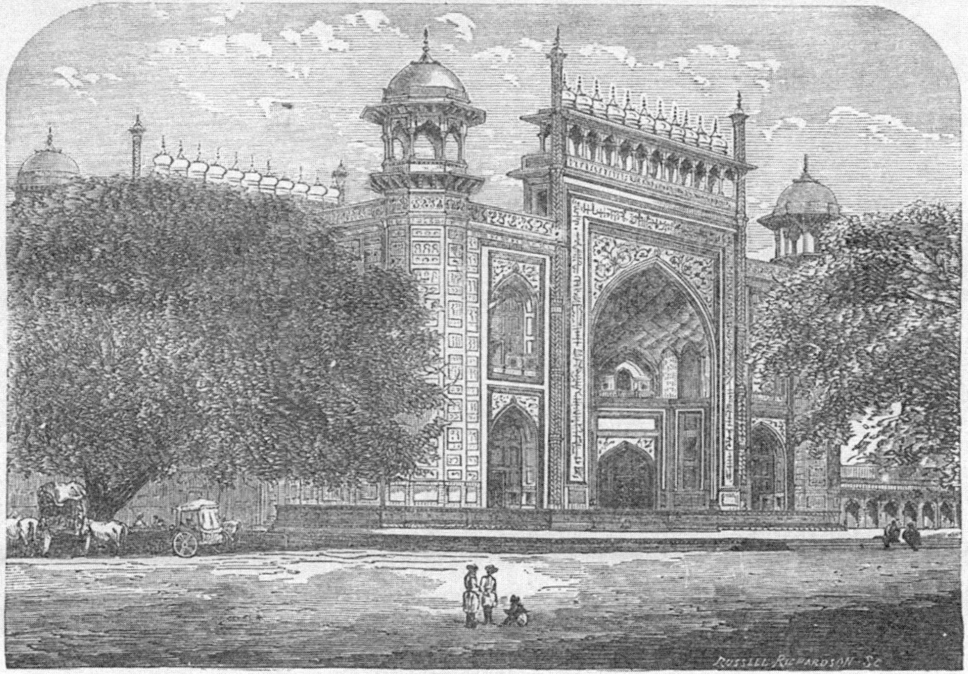

THE GATE OF THE TAJ.

As she concluded Mr. Morgan said, "Why, Miss Thompson, you are eloquent." "No," she replied; "it was only an eloquent subject." Mr. Morgan said, "I should have enjoyed seeing this during the emperor's life-time, when a light from perfumed oil in golden lamps fell upon the tomb day and night, and the choicest of flowers were arranged daily in garlands to adorn it; when the most skillful Mogul musicians filled the air with tenderest strains of melody; when five times every day the muezzin's call to prayer resounded from these minarets, and a eunuch of high station, with two thousand splendidly attired Sepoys, kept guard that no unworthy foot came near."

"But, remember," said Miss Thompson, "if you had then attempted to approach the tomb those Sepoys would have killed you without mercy as a sacrilegious kafir. For my part, I prefer visiting it now, knowing that I am perfectly safe in doing so."

Just then a Mohammedan teacher of the law passed near them, and Mr. Morgan, calling him, asked if he could describe the place to them. The dervish bowed until the ends of his turban touched the ground, then standing erect, with his arms folded, repeated his often-spoken description, as follows:

"The entrance to these spacious gardens is built of red sandstone inlaid with texts from the Koran wrought in white marble. The walls surrounding the garden are of the same material. The gate is in size and beauty a palace, while the arched colonnades running all along the interior of the wall add to the general magnificence of the place. The garden paths are paved with slabs of freestone arranged in fanciful devices. The palms, banyan, bamboo, tamarind, and various fruit-trees are so arranged as to shade the walks, attract the eye, and fill the air with sweetest odors, while the beds of flowers of loveliest hues bloom in profusion, so as to greet the observer's eyes on every hand.

"The central avenue, from the gate to the Taj, is a third of a mile in length, with a marble reservoir in the middle about forty feet square, with five fountains, one in the center and in each corner. There is also a system of fountains, numbering eighty-four, along the paths, and these are bordered by rows of dark Italian cypress-trees. The garden is the resort of many sweet songsters, and is redolent with the odor of roses, oranges, lemons, and tamarind trees.

"The Taj stands upon a double terrace. The first is made of red sandstone, is twenty feet high and a thousand feet broad. On the two extremities of this terrace are two buildings exactly the same in size and shape. The one on the left side is a mosque used for service, as it allows the faces of the worshipers to be set toward the tomb of their prophet at Mecca. The one on the right is a rest-house for the accommodation of visitors who come from various parts of the world to see the Taj, and who here receive free quarters as long as they choose to remain."

"Midway between these two buildings is the second terrace, fifteen feet high and three hundred feet square.

"On the four corners of this terrace stand four minarets. This terrace and the minarets, as also the Taj, which rises up in the center of this square, are of the finest white marble inlaid with jewels. The Taj is square, with truncated corners, and is a hundred and fifty feet in diameter. The dome is seventy feet in diameter, and is two hundred and forty-five feet high. On the top of the dome is a golden spire thirty feet high.

"A Persian manuscript preserved in the Taj gives an account of the stones used in its construction. 'The white marble was brought from Jeypore, the yellow marble from the Nerbudda, the black from Charkoh; the red sandstone from Dholepore; crystal from China; jasper from the Punjab; carnelian from Bagdad; turquoises from Thibet; agate from Temen; lapis lazuli from Ceylon; diamonds from Punah; rock spar from Nerbudda; loadstone from Gwalior; amethyst and onyx from Persia; chalcedony from Villiat, and sapphires from Lauka.'"

As the dervish paused Miss Thompson exclaimed, "Only think that all these materials were brought on elephants or camels, by caravans! What time and labor it must have required!"

The dervish calmly answered, "It required twenty thousand men twenty-two years to build it, and it cost a sum equal to sixty millions of American dollars."

The dervish now led them into the vault below the central hall, where the real sarcophagi, containing the bodies of the emperor and empress, were kept. They then returned to the rotunda, where duplicates of the real sarcophagi were placed directly over the real, and officially representing them. This is the place which for architectural splendor has no equal. The floor is of polished marble and jasper. The wainscoting is of sculptured marble tablets inlaid with flowers formed of precious stones. The windows or screens are of marble filigree richly wrought in various patterns, and admitting only a faint and delicate light into the gorgeous apartment, which is lost in the heights of the lofty dome. The tombs are surrounded by a magnificent octagonal screen about six feet high, with doors on the sides. The open tracery in this white marble screen is wrought into beautiful flowers, such as lilies, irises, and others. The borders of the screen are inlaid with precious stones, representing flowers, executed with such wonderful perfection that the forms wave as in nature, and the hues and shades of the stems, leaves, and flowers appear as real almost as the beauties which they represent. These ornamental designs are so carefully and exquisitely executed that several of the flowers have as many as eighty different stones entering into their composition, all polished uniformly with the marble, into which they are so delicately inserted that you can hardly trace their joinings. They seem as though they had grown there, instead of being separately prepared and placed in their positions by the hands of the "cunning workmen" who designed and executed this imperishable and magnificent memorial of human love. But the richest art is displayed on the cenotaph of the empress within the screen. Upon her tomb, according to universal Mohammedan usage, is a slate or tablet of marble, while on the emperors' is a small box representing a pen-holder. These always distinguish a man's or a woman's grave among these people, the idea being that a woman's heart is a tablet on which lordly man can write whatever pleases him best. And this mark of feminine inferiority was not spared even the beloved occupant of the Taj Mahal.

But her tomb, how beautiful! The snow-white marble is inlaid with flowers so delicately formed that they look like embroidery on white satin, so exquisitely is the mosaic executed in carnelian, bloodstone, agate, jasper, turquois, lapis lazuli, and other precious stones. Thirty-five different specimens of carnelian are employed in forming a single leaf of a carnation; and in one flower, not larger than a silver dollar, as many as twenty-three different stones can be counted. Yet these are but specimens of the beauties that are spread in unparalleled profusion over this entire chamber. Indeed, Long asserts that he found one flower upon her tomb to be composed of no less than three hundred different stones. Her name and date of death, with her virtuous qualities, are recorded in the same costly manner, in gems of Arabic—the sacred language of the Mohammedan—on the side of her tomb. The emperor's tomb is plainer than the other; has no passage from the Koran, but merely a similar mosaic work of flowers and his name, with the date of his death, upon it. Over all this richness and beauty rises the magnificent dome, which is so constructed as to contain an echo more pure, prolonged, and harmonious than any other in the world, so far as known. While they were gazing upon the wonderful beauties of the scene the dervish went into the vault below and began to play on a flute. As the sound rose into the dome, and came back in reverberations from a hundred arched alcoves, it seemed to breathe the notes of angels. It was so delicate, so sweet, so soul-stirring, that no earthly sound exceeded it. It was to the ear what the building was to the eye. It seemed to haunt the distant alcoves of the dome, and to fall upon the listeners in gentle showers. It seemed to merge itself in the soft light of the apartment, and awaken the sweetest fancies in the minds of the hearers. It was the spirit of the Taj; full of love, tenderness, sweetness. Miss Thompson broke the quiet by remarking, "Love was its author, beauty its inspiration." The dervish ceased his playing, led them out of the building, and in silence received his reward and withdrew.

Little was said by the Americans, but, with spirits subdued and tranquilized by the wonderful charm of the place, they thought of the amazing skill that could invent and construct a building expressive of so much sentiment, and capable of arousing in beholders such sympathetic appreciation.

They passed out of the gate, entered their palanquins, and soon arrived in Agra.

As Mr. Morgan bade Miss Thompson good night at the door of the mission house he thought, "The Taj is the most beautiful tribute ever paid a woman's memory by the art of man, but God only can fully reward a woman for her noble life who, like Miss Thompson, has left home, friends, race, and civilization, to be despised, forsaken, ill-treated, and, perhaps, to die, a sacrifice in order to win some poor ignorant souls from a life of sin to the cleansing, helping, saving arms of Jesus. Miss Thompson is nobler and more worthy of honor than Moomtaj-i-Mahal in all her glory."

When Mr. Morgan reached his bungalow he was handed a letter which read as follows:

"DEAR MORGAN: Come to Umballa at once. Every thing is ready—elephants, company, tigers, and all. Bring your splendid American rifle, and prove its value upon tigers. Yours, etc., GREY."

Looking at the train schedule, he saw that he could catch the night train. Packing his baggage and paying his bill, he hastened to the depot. He had just time enough to write a short note to Miss Thompson, explaining his hasty departure, when the cars came rushing into the station. In a few moments the signal was given, and the train was rapidly whirled toward the north-west.

CHAPTER X.

KISMUT.

MOOTIE was a little maiden as happy as the days were long. She was constantly in motion, running, laughing, playing, and pleasing her parents by her bright ways. Like all Hindu maidens, she was very fond of ornaments, and wore a number of rings on her ankles, and arms, in her nose and ears, and necklaces around her throat. She was also fond of ribbons, and gay colors, with which she paraded her taste before the visitors, at her father's home. But her tenth birthday approached, and it would have been a disgrace if her father should not obtain her a husband before another year passed. The time had come for her childhood to end.

Her father proceeded to find a man of the same caste and class, to whom he could marry his little Mootie.

It was not the custom for a girl to have any choice in such a matter, or even to see her husband until the time for the wedding arrived.

Mootie was delighted with the idea of being married. She had seen her sister married, and remembered how joyful the occasion was and how sweet the confectionery tasted.

She would then have a large party and a great feast, and receive new and brilliant clothes; she could put on all her ornaments, and, besides, have many more given her, and, furthermore, would be envied by all the girls with whom she played from earliest childhood. She knew nothing of the awful realities to follow, which she would be doomed to endure.

In choosing a husband for his little daughter, the father might either marry her to some one of suitable age who would take her to his own house, or he might marry her to one of the Brahmans who went about the country marrying girls for a sum of money and then departing, leaving them with their fathers all their lives. Some of these Brahmans in this way would marry as many as a hundred girls, and at his death they would be real widows though they would never see him except on that one occasion. It was an advantage to be allied to the family of a Brahman. It cost less money than the other way, and the father ever after had the advantage of his daughter's service. He also had the pleasure of feeling he had done his duty, and thus retained the respect of his neighbors.

Mootie's sister had been married in this way and another daughter was not needed at home. Mootie was therefore married to a youth of similar caste and clan, who was just twice her age.

The brilliancy of the wedding was all she could desire. So soon as the marriage ceremony was over she bade farewell to parents and friends and went to live in her husband's home, to be trained by his mother to know and satisfy his every wish. This period of tuition would last for a period of six years, when she would be given to her husband to serve him as his wife.

The house to which the little bride was taken, like all Hindu houses of the better sort, was divided into two parts. One of these, the outer, was light and airy, with a broad veranda in front, and a pleasant yard. This was the part occupied by the men.

The inner part was framed for seclusion, being dark and close, without veranda or yard. This was the zenana, or the part occupied by the women. Thus far in her life Mootie had never been restrained, for little children went every-where, but now, as a married person, she was restricted to the zenana, and she sadly learned that the happy marriage was the beginning of a life of toil and privation.

She was now required to be scrupulously exact in all she did or said, and instead of the sweet loving smilesof her mother she saw the stern face and felt the severe blows of the mother-in-law. In a Hindu home the mother-in-law was honored as the ruler of the zenana, and she sustained her position by the most excessive exactions of toil and respect from the other females of the house.

Mootie's life now became a burden, and she shed many tears over her disappointment; but she learned quickly how to cook her husband's food, to anticipate his wants, to serve him at the table, and to observe the proper deportment before him.

She was taught this law from the Shaster: "If a man goes on a journey his wife shall not divert herself by play, nor shall see any public show, nor shall laugh, nor shall dress herself in jewels or fine clothes, nor hear music, nor shall sit at the window, nor shall behold any thing choice and rare, but shall fasten well the house-door, and remain private, and shall not eat any dainty food, and shall not blacken her eyes with powder, and shall not view her face in a mirror; she shall never amuse herself in any such agreeable employment during the absence of her husband."

She was also taught this law: "When in the presence of her husband, a woman should keep her eyes upon her master and be ready to receive his commands. When he speaks she must be quiet, and listen to nothing else besides. When he calls she must leave every thing else and attend upon him alone. A woman has no other god upon earth but her husband. The most excellent of all good works that she can perform is to gratify him with the strictest obedience. This should be her only devotion. Though he be aged, infirm, dissipated, a drunkard, or a debauchee, she must still regard him as her god. She must serve him with all her might, obeying him in all things, spying no defects in his character, and giving him no cause for disquiet. If he laughs, she must

HINDU HUSBAND AND WIFE.

also laugh; if he weeps, she must also weep; if he sings, she must be in an ecstasy."

She was also taught that, if faithful in all things, she would be permitted to go to the same heaven and serve him there; but if unfaithful or negligent she would never enter heaven at all.

Mootie tried to fulfill these conditions, and when the time of her training drew to a close she had the satisfaction of knowing that she could prepare his food to suit him, and could put him to sleep by softly rubbing the soles of his feet with the palms of her hands.

When sixteen years of age, she took her place in serving him as his wife. He was of a kind and generous disposition, and treated her tenderly. He accepted all her services, and being made comfortable by her exertion smiled graciously upon her. She even won his love. Released from the bondage to the mother-in-law the sunshine again came into her life.

She was content to stand near him while he ate, and, when he had finished, to take what he left on his plate into another room and eat it as her portion. She was allowed to again wear ornaments, and decorated *sarees* and other handsome clothes. This pleased him, and was one of the greatest delights of her life.

Mootie was a beautiful young woman. Her eyes were large and expressive. Not with the brightness betokening self-reliance and courage, but a soft, liquid expression, full of tenderness and affection. Her hair, of which she was very proud, was long and glossy, and she bound it around with strings of ornaments. It was the crown to her beauty. She was greatly admired by her husband, and the prospect of a very happy life opened before her.

But, alas! suddenly the bright vision faded, and the dark clouds of adversity rushed upon her pathway.

Her husband came home one day in great pain and weariness, and as she saw the flush on his cheeks she knew he had the fever. She fervently offered her prayers to the gods, bestowed large gifts at their shrines, and nursed him as gently as she could, but all was of no avail. He died.

Her heart was filled with the keenest distress. Gladly would she have followed him to the funeral pyre, and have been burned with him, and thus triumphantly enter heaven by his side; but the laws of the English rulers forbade this sacrifice. She was doomed to pass the rest of her life a Hindu widow, to show by menial service and wretchedness of life the desolate state of her broken career. A Hindu widow is an object of great pity. The beautiful and cheerful Mootie was only seventeen years of age when this sorrow came upon her.

Immediately upon the death of her husband, the

A HINDU WIDOW.

women, led by her mother-in-law, set upon her and cursed her with the most bitter invectives, as being the cause of this awful calamity to their house.

Her fine clothes were stripped from her, and a coarse brown garment, significant of her degradation, was given her. All ornaments, the gifts of her loving husband, were taken from her, for she was never to wear an ornament again. Her beautiful hair was cut off, and her head shaved, and as long as she lived it was to be shaven once every two weeks. She was then given the drudgery of the zenana to do, and allowed only one meal a day. If she rebelled against this she was threatened with severe punishment, and she was continually watched as a desperate thing of evil. She was ordered to remain in close confinement in the zenana, so that no man should see her face and that she should not speak to any one except her nearest relations. If a man should see her he would consider it a bad omen. If she should cross his path in the morning he would turn back to his house. The change was so sudden and terrible that she could hardly realize for a time its full meaning. She was taunted on every hand, deprived of all that made life pleasant, and, utterly crushed by cruel misfortune, knew not what to do. Sometimes the accumulation of miseries made her brain reel.

She thought to escape from the zenana—but what then? No one would receive her. Even the lowest caste people would deny her their friendship; she could only find rest in suicide, or yield to the example of some in embracing a life of shame.

But her mind would not allow her to think seriously of suicide, for the prospect beyond this life was a thousand-fold more horrible than the present. She could not enter a life of shame, because she had always been pure in heart, and no amount of cruelty could drive her to sacrifice her honor. What could she do?

One day the cruel taunts and blows were more than she could bear, and she fled. Having once fled she was afraid to return, so she ran into the jungle to die all alone, or be at the mercy of the wild beasts. Who would have known her as the once handsome Mootie!

Her eyes were red, and cheeks bloated from excessive weeping, her head was shaven and uncovered, and she wore only a single brown gown upon her body, once so plump, but now fast becoming emaciated through deprivation of food. She rushed into the jungle near her home, and with rapid tread pressed on her way. She thought they were pursuing her, and all day she fled, until her feet, bleeding from contact with stones, roots, and thistles, refused to carry her farther. Almost famished she sank helpless to the ground.

When she had rested awhile the instinct of self-preservation aroused her. From a little brook that flowed near by she bathed her wounds, and quenched her thirst. Seeing berries growing by the stream, she plucked them and satisfied the cravings of hunger. As her strength returned, she noticed the light growing dimmer, and that night would soon be upon her with all its horrors. At the thought of the tigers that roamed the jungle she felt a terror almost as great as at the thought of the punishments at home, and she looked for some place in which she might hide from such foes. She soon found an aperture in the rocks, into which she crept, and by wedging stones into the opening from the inside felt secure from foes during the night.

As the darkness became denser the jungle seemed to be filled with millions of insects, which kept up a continual noise. She could not sleep in such strange surroundings, nor could she ward off the mosquitoes that persisted in stinging her with their sharp lances.

Her fear increased when she heard the cry of a hungry tiger scenting her from afar. As he came nearer she wedged the stones the tighter in the opening of her retreat. With eager ferocity he put his nose to the rocks, sniffed the atmosphere laden with her breath, then gave a roar that resounded throughout the jungle, and almost made poor Mootie mad with fright. It was so loud and fierce that it seemed to shake the rocks about her. She felt against her cheeks the hot glow of his breath coming through the interstices between the stones. Then with his great claws he scratched the stones, and growled with rage as he failed to move them.

Sometimes he would lie down, and with both paws try to remove the stones, then he would get up and walk to and fro, growling savagely all the time. Then he would strike at the stones to push them from their places. But Mootie did not move. She hardly dared breathe. With stiffened muscles she pressed her weight upon the props, keeping the stones in their places. And with pitiful yearning prayed for the coming of the day. She did not think of her aching hands or her bleeding feet, and the noise and stings of the mosquitoes no longer distressed her: she only thought of escaping from that terrible tiger.

At length the streaks of dawn began to appear, and the tiger, after one last effort to capture the prey so near him, left the spot and retreated to his lair until darkness should again enable him to come forth. She heard his loud growling as he went away, and then, unable to longer endure the strain, fell into a deep sleep. She was awakened by the sound of voices, and perceived men standing before her retreat. As they spoke she recognized them as the men of her village. They had tracked her thus far and were conversing about her fate. Listening, she could hear their words.

They saw the marks of her blood upon the ground and the stones, but they also saw the marks of the tiger's tongue as he had tried to lick up the drops of blood. They saw pieces of her gown torn by the thorn-bushes through which she had pressed her way. They saw the foot-prints of the tiger in the soft earth and the place where he had rolled in his anger. The evidence to them was plain—she had been eaten by the tiger.

One of them said, "That is her fate." She listened until they were out of hearing, and thought, "Now I am dead to them all. They will never look for me again. I will be a new person. I will have a new name. They said it is my 'fate.' Fate shall be my name. I will be Kismut.* Mootie was eaten by the tiger, but Kismut will come out of the rocks."

With such thoughts she left her retreat, bathed again in the brook, ate some berries, and, with a happier heart than she had known since her husband's death, plunged deeper into the jungle.

* *Kismut* is the Mohammedan word meaning fate.

CHAPTER XI.

MORGAN SHOOTS THE TIGER.

WHEN Edward Morgan reached the rendezvous he found the entire party present, and awaiting his arrival to proceed on their hunt. The people of that village and those neighboring were in a state of unusual excitement. They represented that the jungle was full of tigers, they told of children being caught by tigers when playing in the street of the village; and every one was telling how the widow Mootie was carried by a tiger into the jungle and devoured; that the savage beast had even licked up all the drops of blood she shed except in a few places in the crevices of the rocks where he made his feast.

The villagers gladly welcomed the huntsmen, and called upon their gods to give them success in ridding their country of the ferocious beasts.

The universal excitement made the hunters feel quite heroic; but Captain Grey suggested that in reality there were probably not more than a pair of tigers, as they usually foraged in pairs.

Before starting they engaged the services of a guide, an experienced hunter, who gave them instructions how to hunt. He said: "There are three kinds of tigers, or, rather, stages in a tiger's life. The young tiger, living a free, wild life in the depths of the jungle, afraid of man, not strong enough to master buffaloes, contents itself with living on smaller game and keeping in solitude. These are not much more than kittens—they lack experience. As they become older and get stronger they rove in companies, and learn from their older companions to attack large animals. They also prowl about the borders of the villages, picking up a sheep or a calf, and after a while attacking a full-grown bullock. They learn to relish domesticated flesh as choicer, daintier food than that of wild animals, and easier to obtain. They dread the face of man, however, and only in a sneaking way perform their robberies. But being often chased by men they become bolder, and even stop to fight for the possession of their plunder, and in this way get a taste of human blood. From this moment the tiger is a new creature. Human blood intoxicates him. He thirsts for it with such intensity that he will not be satisfied with any thing less. He will at times watch the highways and, in daylight even, spring upon the traveler. He will rush into a village and seize a child and carry it off before the horror-stricken people can prevent. His ferocity becomes terrible. These man-eating tigers are generally of full age and mangey. They possess tremendous strength and are hard to overcome. When one enters a neighborhood universal consternation prevails, and there is no sense of security until he is killed. But it often happens that many lives are lost before this is accomplished."

Those who had searched for Mootie declared that the beast that carried her away was old and large; one of the most dangerous kind. They knew it from the size of his foot-prints and the marks of his claws on the trees.

There were three ways of hunting the tiger. One way was to construct a house or cage of bamboo near his haunt, to place a sheep in the lower part and thus attract him by its bleating; while the hunters in the upper part, protected from his approach, could deliberately shoot him as he came near. Another way was to hunt him with elephants. The hunter, with his ammunition and weapons, safely stowed in a howdah on the elephant's back was out of danger, although the driver, sitting on the elephant's neck to direct him, was in danger of the tiger springing upon him and tearing him from his place. The only danger to the hunter was that sometimes an elephant became frightened and uncontrollable, and would rush among the trees, tearing the howdah from his back and thoroughly wrecking it. The other way of hunting, and the most dangerous way, was to approach the tiger on foot; then the hunter put his skill fairly against that of the beast. This required the greatest care, the firmest nerve, and the surest weapons. A weakness in either of these meant death.

When the guide had explained these features of the

hunt, Morgan declared that when they came near the tiger's haunt he would hunt him on foot. The people gazed upon him in astonishment at this statement, and yet with admiration of his bold spirit. He called for some native hunters to support him, and immediately at least a dozen brave, stalwart men, with only a cloth about their loins, turbans on their heads, and spears in their hands, stepped forth, ready to follow him wherever he might lead.

Elephants were now led before the dwelling of the chief man of the village, and provisions for many days were packed in the howdahs; the provisions consisting mostly of various kinds of canned goods and unleavened crackers, with meal of different kinds. A good stock of ammunition was also put in the howdahs, and then the hunters mounted to their places.

The starting of the hunters caused the day to be made a gala day by the villagers. Many came from neighboring villages to see them and wish them success. While it meant sport to the party it meant security to the villages, and yet every one knew that it might mean death to some of the hunters; for an old tiger was always very dangerous. The elephants were covered with gay-colored cloths, while passing through the villages, and the hunters held their weapons up bound about with ribbons and flowers. The people were dressed in their brightest colored clothing, and were decorated with all their jewelry. With shouts, blowing of horns, beating of pans, and every imaginable kind of noise they sent the party on their way.

Such an ovation made the beginning seem like a triumphal march, and Morgan entered into the spirit of it in true, frank, free American manner. He said it led him to think of the Fourth of July. Dennis also imbibed the spirit of the occasion. His tongue ran continually, to the merriment of the people. With red face, broad brogue, and ardent gestures he loudly boasted of what they would do, and to each of his promises the people beat their tom-toms the louder. Then the party left the villages and plunged into the jungle. They proceeded at a rapid pace for several miles, the native hunters running by the side of the elephants. At length the guide called a halt, and showed them where the tiger had wallowed at the foot of a tree, and had torn the bark of the tree by his clawing. As he examined it, he said, "The tiger was in a rage when he did this; his strokes are deep and uneven. He is a ferocious fellow, and we must be careful of him." Then showing them the broad foot-prints in the earth, they took up their journey more slowly, tracking him toward his lair. In some places it was difficult to follow him, for he seemed to prefer running in the brook, and leaping from side to side as if to conceal his tracks. After traveling in this way for a couple of hours the guide announced the discovery of the tracks of another tiger, also a large one. The excitement was now intense, and every one prepared for the combat. Morgan alighted from his elephant, and, having first carefully examined his fine Springfield rifle, started with his native hunters on foot to find the lair of the tiger. The others, remaining on their elephants, sought the tracks in the more open parts of the jungle. Each party took a separate route, so as to surround the thicket in which the guide declared the tigers were concealed. The tiger's haunt was supposed to be in a dense bamboo thicket just before them, and it was possible that the beast might spring upon the hunters before its presence would be discovered.

The elephants tramped about the thicket, while the native hunters, with their spears carefully poised, entered the dangerous precincts. Morgan seemed to coolly take it as an every-day occurrence, but in reality he was intensely excited. This was the greatest hunt of his life, and its issue would distinguish him in the estimation of his companions or load him with discredit. Suddenly the hunter in front of him ceased his advance, and standing perfectly upright pointed with his spear to a small open space within the thicket.

Looking in the direction indicated, Morgan saw a tiger not thirty yards distant; the first tiger he ever beheld at liberty. It was a thrilling sight, for the beast saw them, and was angry at their approach. He was in the act of devouring a buffalo, which he had dragged to his lair. They saw him plunge into the reeking flesh, then raising his head, dripping with gore, he glared savagely at his enemies and growled fiercely. Then, seeming to realize his danger, he left the carcass and walked about it, uttering his rage in a succession of roars.

He was an immense beast, and as he moved about, with so soft and graceful a motion, Morgan could not refrain from admiring the velvety stripes of black on his soft golden coat. But the time for action had come. Raising his rifle to his shoulder he took a quick aim at the monster and fired. He struck the tiger but did not mortally wound him, and only increased the animal's rage. Now came a moment of the greatest danger, which severely tested the courage of them all. But not one sought safety in flight; every one stood erect in his place, depending for his life on the skill of their leader. Instantly he reloaded, as the tiger, with a roar that was the most terrifying sound Morgan ever heard, sprang forward.

Morgan's rifle was again at his shoulder as the tiger crouched for its final spring, and a second of time would decide the death either of the hunter or of the beast.

If Morgan should miss his aim, or his motion be too slow, or his ball strike the wrong curve of the animal's skull, or his rifle hang fire, the tiger would be upon him with its awful teeth and claws. The men saw the danger, but not a man stirred. Morgan stood erect, without a tremor, one foot a little in advance of the other, with his eye along the gun-barrel. The tiger sprang! at the same instant the report of the rifle rang out, the ball went straight on its course through the eye of the beast into the brain, and the huge body fell at the feet of the hunter, quivering in the throes of death. It was several moments before the death agonies were over, when they could safely approach the body of the tiger. Then Morgan with an exultation new to him, a joyous pride that almost made him laugh and cry by turns, went up to the beast, and with his hands stroked its sleek sides, handled its immense paws, and felt its claws and then its teeth while the body was yet warm with the lately coursing heat of life. The native hunters came up to him and with expressions of reverence bowed before him. They called him a great hunter, whose skill and courage had never been surpassed.

But they were not alone in their praises. Captain Grey's elephant had come up just as the first shot was fired, and he and Dennis had witnessed the whole action. The awful danger Morgan stood under for the moment unnerved the captain, and now as he took Morgan's hand to congratulate him he was unable to utter a word. He could only heartily grasp the hand of his friend, while the tears rolled down his cheeks. Morgan understood it, and it bound him to Grey with the strongest links of friendship. Dennis danced about the beast with uncontrollable delight. His eyes sparkled, and his entire countenance was illuminated with the peculiar Irish glow as he said to the native hunters, "Look at that now! Did yez iver see the bate o' that? 'twas a brave deed Mister Morgan did, an' niver a bit o' fear in his eye at all, at all. Whisht now, but war'n't it purty how he so nately decaved the ould monster?" Then turning to the carcass, he continued: "An' did yez think to make a dinner of the likes o' him, ye brute ye! Sure an' 'tis not for the likes of yez to feast upon American beef." Then blushing he bowed and said, "that is to say, as it were, an American gintleman of unexcelled excellence, and the possesser of the best of vartues."

By this time the other hunters arrived, and they proceeded to dispose of the beast. He was pronounced to be a ferocious man-eater, and was nearly ten feet in length. They skinned the carcass, and with chemicals they had brought with them prepared the skin, with the head and claws, for preservation. Morgan wished to send it to America as a proof of his ability as a huntsman. Then, building a fire, they prepared a sumptuous dinner, after which they resumed their search for the other tiger.

CHAPTER XII.

WHAT ELEPHANTS CAN DO.

THE slaughter of the tiger without any accident to the party stimulated them to press the search for the other one with vigor. Even the elephants manifested this desire by their trumpeting and snorting. The guide, however, cautioned watch care, for the tiger would sell his life dearly. In a short time they marked his trail and followed it into a dense thicket along a stream that ran through the jungle. The elephants now seemed to be more wary, and at times almost hesitated to proceed. Suddenly they were all alarmed by the tiger, just in front of them, uttering a tremendous roar and springing at the neck of the nearest elephant. With his huge claw he tore from beneath the driver a part of the pad on which he sat, and would have pulled him off if Dennis had not caught the frightened man by the shoulder and held him on.

They all hastened to shoot at the beast, but he retired so quickly into the thicket that none of their shots took effect. The elephant, however, seemed to be very angry with the liberties the tiger had taken. The full view which the party had of the motions of the great beast awakened their admiration. Beauty, grace, power, and ferocity were combined, and with it all there seemed to be a degree of skill in his method of attack worthy of the reason of man. They could not see where he had gone, so dense was the thicket and so silently did he await their approach. The very air seemed still, and only the lumbering crash of the elephant's step disturbed the awful quiet.

This silence was very aggravating to Dennis, and at last, as he stood in the edge of the howdah with rifle in hand watching the thicket, he began to mutter imprecations upon the foe. His remarks were suddenly cut short, however, by the elephant making a sudden move backward upon his haunches with such force as to throw Dennis to the ground. He was not hurt, however, and, realizing his danger, quickly arose and stood with his rifle ready for action. But his attention was directed to the elephant, for it was now taking an active part in the fray.

The elephant had seen considerable service in tiger-hunting, and was highly valued for his courage and strength. He was of a great age and thoroughly trained, but sometimes he became a little impatient when things did not progress to suit him. He had a pair of enormous tusks, which added to his fierce appearance as well as to his strength. From the moment the tiger dared to leap upon him and lacerate his shoulder with its terrible claws his indignation had been increasing, and, watching the retreat of his foe, he suddenly caught sight of the glossy yellow and black far in the thicket. Throwing himself on his haunches, as if to get command of his great muscular force—the movement which threw Dennis to the ground—he rushed with furious energy into the thicket with his head bent down toward the ground. Nothing could withstand the force of that assault. The howdah and all who were in it were swept from his back by the branches of intervening trees. The bamboo reeds of the thicket were broken and trampled down as if they were only straws. The astonished hunters saw him drive his tusks toward the ground with awful fury, and the next moment he came out of the thicket with the tiger hanging on the tusks and pierced through by them both. Then grasping the tiger with his trunk he hurled him from the tusks to the ground, and never ceased his fury until he had trampled the body to a mass of gore and pulp. Then, seeing his enemy was thoroughly destroyed and his own honor vindicated, he yielded to the commands of his driver, and became gentle again.*

The men so suddenly swept from his back were magnanimous enough to forgive his treatment of them and to praise his courage and strength of will in the most ardent terms. Dennis beheld the entire action. It was all so quickly done that he did not have a chance to even shoot at the tiger, and he was

* This action of an elephant actually occurred.

disappointed that the hunt should close and not a bit of glory accrue to himself.

The tigers were now destroyed in that part of the jungle, and the rest of the hunting was tame. There were buffaloes, wild hogs, antelopes, and other game which they could easily slaughter, but the real sport was ended, and they returned to the village with the skins of the slain tigers, and received the generous ovation which the grateful villagers hastened to give them.

The entire party, with the exception of Morgan, then started for the nearest railway station to return to their various quarters.

On the road Morgan left them, to pass through the jungle to intersect the great highway to the north-west, and to enjoy the luxury of solitude amidst unusual dangers. He chose to go alone. He had been traveling for several hours, and was considerably fatigued, when, on reaching an elevated piece of ground, he saw a short distance before him the broad highway. The great road is sixteen hundred miles long, made of concrete, and as hard and smooth as a floor. It is said by a great bicycler, who went around the world on his bicycle, to be the finest road in the world.

Previous to the mutiny the roads in India were poor, and on that distressing occasion one great difficulty was to move the troops with sufficient speed. Since then the English have developed the highway.

All along the country there is an abundance of the best concrete, and hence the construction of good highways has not been very difficult. Nowhere in the world have the customs of the people more imperatively demanded good roads than in India; for caste rules largely demand solitary traveling. Palanquins are therefore a neccessity. In these the high caste Hindu, the proud Brahman, the noble lady, or the invalid could travel in safety, free from contact with those of other castes and free from the gaze of strangers. Along the highways were travelers' bungalows, or houses where the traveler could cook his own food, sleep on his own mat or bed, and be by himself as much as he pleased. The traveler always carried in his palanquin every thing necessary for his comfort. So scrupulous were they that they would run no risks by defiling themselves with the things of strangers.

In the distance Morgan saw one of these bungalows, with its whitewashed walls and broad verandas. This was where he expected to pass the night. It was only two or three miles away, and he could soon walk that distance. In the other direction he saw a party of travelers approaching. There were several palanquins, and they were traveling in haste. Morgan watched them as they passed along, Each palanquin was suspended from long poles and carried on the shoulders of four coolies. These coolies changed with relays at regular periods, so that quite a long distance could be passed over in a day. Their uniform swinging step was very graceful, and gave the gentlest rocking motion to the palanquins, very pleasant to those riding.

The palanquins were now near enough for Morgan to see that some persons of considerable importance were in them. They were richly ornamented with bright cloths and jewels, and the curtains were handsomely embroidered. The coolies carried them with a skill demanded by those who possessed authority. But the curtains were tightly drawn, and the riders could not be seen.

Suddenly the ease of their motion was broken, and they came to a halt. The cause of this was apparent to Morgan, for at that moment he heard the snorting of an elephant coming down the highway approaching them. The sound was peculiar, and at once the cry arose from the coolies, "Rogue elephant! Rogue elephant!"

On came the elephant until he was in sight of the travelers. The coolies in abject terror dropped their palanquins and fled to the thickets on the far side of the highway. The curtains of the foremost palanquin parted and a man in brilliant attire stepped out. Morgan noticed that he was a man of authority, and that his dress, sword, jewels, and general bearing showed that he was accustomed to command. But it was too late for him to escape; the huge furious beast rushed upon him, seized him with his trunk dashed him to the ground, and trampled upon him. Some of the coolies who had turned to the defense of their master next became victims of the elephant's rage, and were tossed and trampled to death. Then the beast's rage was directed upon the palanquin, which was soon wrecked.

In the meantime the second palanquin was opened, and a lady, brilliantly dressed, leaped out and ran across the highway toward the hill upon which Morgan was resting. She was evidently trying to reach a tree, with low branches, that stood a short distance from the road-side.

As Morgan, with rifle ready for use started to assist the ill-fated travelers, the beast saw the woman fleeing, and leaving the wreck rushed after her.

He advanced with gigantic strides, holding his head high and his proboscis curled up tightly, in front of his mouth, ready to be swung out with swift precision when near enough to catch his foe. His gigantic tusks pointed almost straight before him, and he threatened to annihilate every thing that stood in his way.

He was gaining rapidly on the lady, although she was fleeing with a speed utterly amazing to the American. The elephant had almost come up to her, when she reached the tree, leaped up, caught hold of a branch, and with wonderful muscular effort swung herself into the higher branches.

Then the elephant's rage was terrific. He plowed deep furrows in the ground with his tusks, and tore off the limbs within his reach with his trunk; but the woman, far above him, watched his vain rage with a feeling of temporary security.

Then the beast caught sight of the American, and with redoubled rage rushed toward him. Edward Morgan was no coward, but in all his life he had never faced such a foe as this. It was like the rush of a railway train. He knew the skull of an elephant could be easily pierced by his powerful Springfield rifle if he could hit the skull. But, in his onward rush, the beast, holding his head up, presented a great mass of flesh which no bullet would affect. It was absolutely necessary to get a partial side view of the animal. Only when the animal was close to him could this be done, and then it might be too late.

The woman in the tree beheld the danger of the hunter, and with quick action sprang out of the tree to the ground. She tore off her brilliant scarlet *saree*, and with a shout flung it toward the beast. The noise and the bright object caught the animal's attention, and without lessening his speed, he partially turned his head toward the maiden. That was enough; the same second the rifle spoke, and the ball whizzed into the brain of the beast, and he fell upon his tusks, rolled over, and died.

As the woman recovered her *saree* Morgan caught a view of her face, and his heart thrilled with glad surprise, for he recognized Nemorama, the beautiful nautchnee. His countenance revealed his delight, and as he called her name she recognized him, and with no less delight came at his call. As she gazed into his face and read its expression the thought of her destination flashed upon her, filling her mind with terror, and, looking appealingly into his eyes, she said: "O, stranger, you have risked your life to save me! You have indeed saved my life! O, will you save me from a fate worse than death? O, let us flee into the jungle before I am sought by those holding me captive, and as soon as we are safe from pursuit I will tell you all."

Morgan did not need a second appeal. As he gazed into her beautiful, beseeching face, radiant with feeling and hope, he remembered the fakir's story, and he replied: "I will save you, beautiful one, or will die in the attempt. Come with me. The coolies have fled in the other direction, and have not observed your flight. Me they have not seen. We will soon cover our tracks in the streams of the jungle, and they will think you are dead." He led the way, and they quickly passed into the jungle. There were many thickets interspersed here and there with little streams, patches of swamp, and high tufts of grass. In and out among these tufts they rapidly fled until they reached drier ground, and upon this they continued their flight until darkness settled upon them. But they felt secure, for they were many miles away from any who might seek for them. While waiting for daylight they climbed into the branches of a bushy tree, to be safe from the beasts that roamed the jungle during the darkness.

When the coolies recovered their courage they hastened to the nearest village, and with men and torches returned to the scene of carnage. Great was their consternation on seeing the havoc done. Their master and his body-guard were so crushed as to be distinguished only by their clothing and ornaments. The palanquins were wrecked and the fragments scattered along the highway. The lady they were bearing was gone, with no trace of her flight, and the elephant that had wrought all this mischief lay dead beneath a badly broken tree. They wondered if the elephant died in a fit. But their great perplexity was as to the fate of the lady. Sadly they gathered the bodies of the slain and placed them upon funeral pyres, and committed them to the flames. With torches they searched for traces of the lady, but just there the ground was covered with grass and no foot-prints were seen. They at last gave up the search and returned to the bungalow to wait for daylight. In the night they heard the fierce cries of the wild hyenas, and in the morning they found these savage, hungry beasts had fought over the body of the elephant, and there had been so many of them that only a mass of bones, with the two great tusks, was left.

Sure that the lady must have perished in the same way, they went on their journey. A Mahommedan fakir, following them from the bungalow, picked up a bullet from the skull of the elephant and hid it in his hair.

CHAPTER XIII.

LIGHT IN THE JUNGLE.

THE tree in which the fleeing ones sought shelter was bushy with branches, the forks of which afforded them easy and safe resting-places. The branches grew so thickly that there was no danger of their falling to the ground, even if sleep should overcome them.

During the first part of the night they kept silence, thinking to avoid attracting the attention of any thing that might endanger their safety. They forgot that wild animals are attracted by scent more than by noise or sight. The darkness was intense. On every hand the jungle seemed to be alive with myriads of insects which kept up a continual humming and buzzing. Occasionally cries of panthers were heard, suggesting the possibility of one of these nimble creatures springing upon them in spite of every precaution. Hyenas and jackals, crying, barking, and fighting, rushed in packs beneath the tree, making the darkness hideous with their savage noises.

Morgan sat in a fork of the tree just above his companion, with his rifle resting on his knee ready for instant action, full of courage in feeling the responsibility he had assumed as her protector.

As the hours passed so slowly and they became

accustomed to the darkness and the strange sounds about them, they began to converse in low tones, which were now and then interrupted by fierce barks from some animals on the ground beneath them disappointed in not finding them their prey.

Naturally their conversation drifted to their first meeting, and Morgan told the maiden that what first really awakened a particular interest in her was the melancholy flashing of her countenance while personating the heroine in Rama's drama. He felt that it was not all art, but a real picture of the hopeless grief she was enduring in her own soul.

Then he told her of the fakir and his story. As he proceeded he noticed that she was weeping. Reaching his hand down to her and touching her shoulder, he discovered that she was trembling with overwhelming excitement. He realized that he was opening to her a glimpse of her own identity, and showing her that she was not a mere thing, but somebody's loved child, and not the child of shame—that her right was of honorable and high caste parentage.

It was the first intelligence she had ever received regarding her parentage, and it explained to some extent the possession of such ardent longings for a better life. With this knowledge sprang into action a desire to find her father, and the probability of his being alive became a rock to rest her hope upon. She told her companion how the ambition to be somebody in life had possessed her whole soul, and she anticipated with a feeling akin to terror living as a mere piece of machinery, for the gratification of the heartless multitudes about her. She told him how all ambition was crushed out of the hearts of the girls, and they were led to be nerveless and depraved by being taught that they were no better than animals; that they were a curse to men, and could never rise in the scale of life; that they were not fit to think for themselves, and should be entirely satisfied in being allowed to wear ornaments and gay colored garments.

Beyond this many of them had no thought, and eternity was a dark cloud. They knew nothing of future blessings and the forgiveness of sins. They lived in moral gloom. She never had received even a ray of light or hope until the American missionary told of the love of Jesus at the bedside of the dying nautchnee, Saineh. She had not heard it since, although the sweetness of the message made her heart-hunger the more apparent and hopeful. Her soul seemed to be in a famishing condition, hungering and thirsting for more of that sweet story of grace and salvation in Jesus.

As Nemorama so touchingly described her heart-hunger, Morgan thought of the opportunities he had carelessly rejected. He had been surrounded from infancy with beams of clearest light from God's throne, and yet had never praised the Giver of that light, nor opened the door of his heart for its entrance. The maiden's yearnings awakened his conscience. He recalled the irrepressible enthusiasm manifested by the missionaries on shipboard; their deep longing to give light to the spiritually blind, the joy they felt when they heard of the heathen accepting the light, and their hope that God would use them as light-bearers. He had pitied the missionaries, and at times considered them deluded fanatics, but now he felt impressed with the duty of doing their kind of work. A soul was calling to him out of the darkness of heathenism. What would he do? What could he say? He was overwhelmed with the thought of his own unworthiness. He beheld the missionary sphere to be so far above his sphere of life that only the special dispensation of heavenly grace could fit him for it.

The thought flashed into his mind that God had delivered him from the tiger and the elephant to use his talents in proclaiming the word of salvation. He bent his soul before God in humble prayer for wisdom to speak it aright. As they were both silent for a while his mind went back over the past. As he reflected, memory brought before him the story of Jesus as he had learned it when a little boy begging his mother for stories. She had entertained him night after night with the gentle words and kind deeds of Jesus. Page after page of literature he had read, sermon after sermon that he had heard, and many other influences he had been subject to came before him, until he was amazed to find how greatly Christ had entered into the warp and woof of his mind. He thought he would give the maiden an historical sketch of Jesus—that was about all he was competent to do. It would interest her, and satisfy the demands of his own conscience. He began, but as he realized she was becoming deeply interested, and drinking in the words as a fever-stricken person would drink fresh spring-water, he gave a bright coloring to his words, until with all the wealth of his cultivated and poetic mind he was presenting to her Christ the Saviour of the lost. Never before was he so deeply affected by his own words as now. His heart opened to the call of his mind, and while the darkness rested on them without, the most wonderful light he had ever known was breaking upon his soul. He began with the story of the heavenly kingdom, where the Son dwelt with the Father and received the adoration of the angels. Then told of the creation of man, and that all people are of one blood and all are the children of God; Sudra as well as Brahman, Asiatic as well as American, woman as well as man. He described the Garden of Eden, and sin entering that garden to lure mankind to ruin; the fall of man, and the punishment God sent upon the offenders. Then he spoke of Christ laying aside his glory and coming to the earth, seeking to save poor lost humanity by the sacrifice of his own blood. He told her how he was received; of the Marys, of the home in Bethany, of the crucifixion, the resurrection, the ascension, the enthronement on high. Then he described the coming judgment and the eternal rewards for the good, and the punishments for the wicked. He spoke particularly of Christ's bearing toward women, and the effect Christianity has had upon the life of women, contrasting happy, free America with suffering India.

The message of life filled Nemorama's heart to overflowing, and she wept for gladness to know Christ would save her. As she wept Morgan turned his thoughts upon himself. He had come to the jungle to hunt the fierce and terrible tiger, and had found the sweet and gentle Christ. In his gladness he recognized the fact; that in trying to show Christ to another he was able to perceive him himself; that in declaring the glad tidings his own ear, listening, caught the message and refused to let it go. He saw how sympathy with one in darkness revealed the fact of his own darkness, and the possibility of one in dense darkness receiving the light made it plain to his own soul that, always having had the light, it was time to acknowledge that the light should be the life of his own soul.

In America he had only thought of Christ as a good man and a great teacher, embodying the deep cravings of humanity, and specially gifted in voicing those cravings, with assurances to satisfy them. Now, however, surrounded by heathenism, he saw how the world needed Christ, and without him was indeed lost. He became more anxious that Nemorama should fully grasp the truth, and all the night, even until the day dawned, while the wolves barked and the jackals uttered their cries, he told over and over again the sweet story of redemption. As the dawn broke upon the jungle, and the wild beasts fled to their lairs, both of them yielded to weariness and slept. When Morgan awoke the full light of the morning was beaming upon him. Looking around him he saw his fair companion, snugly supported by the thick branches in deep slumber. Her head was resting on a friendly limb that formed the pillow, her lips were parted just enough to reveal the beauty of her teeth; her fine mass of hair was bound into a knot on the back of her head, forming a protection from the hardness of the limb. Her *saree* was thrown partly aside, revealing the rich color of her neck. One arm, as if to prevent her from falling, was thrown over the limb, the other was resting on her breast; both of them revealing the beauty and muscular solidity so prized in a nautchnee.

The Hindus, being an Aryan race, have the same facial formation as the Europeans or Americans, and their complexion is but a shade darker; hence their type of beauty is about the same. Nemorama, being half English, was fairer in complexion than the Hindus, and yet more richly tinged than the Europeans. As Morgan gazed upon her, watching the gentle motion of her breast and the calm, sweet confident peace of her face, he thought of Shelley's words:

> "How wonderful is Death!
> Death and his brother, Sleep!
> One, pale as yonder waning moon,
> With lips of lurid blue;
> The other, rosy as the morn
> When, throned on ocean's wave,
> It blushes o'er the world:
> Yet both so passing wonderful!
> Hath then the gloomy Power
> Whose reign is in the tainted sepulchers
> Seized on her sinless soul?
> Must then that peerless form
> Which love and admiration cannot view
> Without a beating heart, those azure veins
> Which steal like streams along a field of snow,
> That lovely outline which is fair
> As breathing marble, perish?
> Or is it only a sweet slumber
> Stealing o'er sensation,
> Which the breath of roseate morning
> Chaseth into darkness?
> Will Ianthe wake again,
> And give that faithful bosom joy
> Whose sleepless spirit waits to catch
> Light, life, and rapture from her smile?
> Yes! she will awake again,
> Although her glowing limbs are motionless,
> And silent those sweet lips
> Once breathing eloquence
> That might have soothed a tiger's rage,
> Or thawed the cold heart of a conqueror."

For a while he continued to gaze upon her, his heart filling with throes of love; then, unwilling that she should awake and see him thus enamored, he took his rifle and noiselessly dropped to the ground. All about the tree were bushes with quantities of ripe berries upon them, save where the beasts of the night had trampled them as they rushed to and fro. Morgan knew that the Hindus did not eat meat; they were vegetarians, and had a sort of horror of flesh-eaters. But he wanted something with more substance than berries, and as there were great droves of wild hogs in the forest he determined to have a nice steak for breakfast.

He had gone but a short distance from the tree, and was looking about him to judge the best course to take when his attention was attracted by a person rapidly moving along on the other side of the bushes from him. It was a person with a head shaved like a Hindu's, with loins girt like a coolie's, with soft and fair-looking flesh, with beautiful countenance and graceful motions. In one hand she carried a stout club, evidently a weapon of defense, while with the other hand she plucked the luscious berries and ate them. She passed along until she came to the tree where the nautchnee was sleeping. There she stopped, looked as if horrified, then turned to flee. Morgan saw Nemorama descending from the tree, and this had frightened the stranger. Determined to solve the mystery of this person he rushed from his hiding-place and caught her in his arms. As he did so she screamed with fright, and struggled so hard to be free that he had to use all his strength to hold her. It did not occur to him that she might be a Hindu of high caste, and that the touch, even, of a stranger was dreadful pollution; but with all her fear she remembered her caste, and the thought of the pollution was greater than her fear.

At length she ceased to struggle, and, quieting her alarm with gentle words, he led her to the astonished Nemorama. Nemorama motioned Morgan to retire to a short distance while she sought to soothe the strange woman. With gentle words and caresses she pacified her. Taking off her own *saree* she threw it over the shoulders of the stranger, and, as if with an excess of kindness, took one of the handsome necklaces from her own neck and placed it on the stranger. Such kindness was irresistible, and, bursting into tears, the stranger wept convulsively. When she had mastered her emotions she told the story of her life, and ended by saying, "And now my name is Kismut."

When Morgan returned Nemorama told him the story of his prisoner, and he then told them the story of the tiger-hunting. Kismut was greatly interested in the remarks the people made about her, extolling her virtues when they supposed her to be dead. She pleaded that they would not reveal the fact of her being alive, but take her with them, and she would faithfully serve them wherever they might go. She took them to the cave in which she had found shelter since coming into the jungle. It was a hole in the rocks, which she had fortified by pieces of stone so as to afford protection against the prowling beasts of the jungle. Her only fear was of serpents, and her only tormentors were the monkeys. The jungle seemed to swarm with monkeys. In great troups they came to her den, and, with incessant chatterings, made the most hideous grimaces at her. But when she shook her stick at them they fled into the neighboring tree-trops. They would steal every thing they could find when she was out of the cave, but when she was there they kept at a distance. At first she was greatly alarmed by them, but she had learned that they were harmless, and, moreover, she had been taught that they were sacred, so she laughed at their antics and felt a degree of companionship in their presence. Without them the jungle would have been very lonesome.

By this time the morning was far advanced, and, as they had endured so much since partaking of food, they began to feel the pangs of hunger. Kismut led them where the berries were the most luscious and plentiful, but Morgan, used to meat, left them to try again if he could find the kind of food he craved.

CHAPTER XIV.

FINDING THE TRAIL.

As Morgan went deeper into the jungle in search of animals fit for food, he reflected on the peculiar situation into which he had drifted. Here he was, a young man, an entire stranger to the customs of the country, ignorant of most of the dialects spoken by the people, with no sympathy for the prevailing religious opinions, having two beautiful young women, both refugees, alone with him in the jungle.

With knowledge of their past lives, and the cause of their being refugees, he had intelligently and willingly become their protector. Now that he had become their guardian, what should he do with them? They might at any time be intercepted by hunters, fakirs, or government officials. They might be attacked by tigers, panthers, bears, wolves or hyenas. They might fall victims to the jungle fever—in fact, it was probable that they would if they remained very long in the jungle. Hence it was necessary to leave the jungle just as soon as they could with safety.

But how?

It was not an easy matter to return to civilization. Being an American, his appearing in any village would awaken general comment, and every one would be curious to see him. Then some one might recognize his companions, and, even if they were not known, the fact of two Hindu women accompanying a foreigner would arouse public inquiries which might be exceedingly annoying. If he could get to the railroad he might soon be hundreds of miles away, but how to get to the railroad was the perplexing question.

As he walked down the bank of the jungle stream he saw in the distance a small column of smoke rising above the trees. The sight startled him, and he determined to discover the cause of it. After walking quite a distance he saw, on the bank of the stream, a small hut well sheltered from observation by the thick growth of trees surrounding it.

Sitting on the ground by the door of the hut was an old and weather-beaten fisherman, engaged in mending a net.

Morgan silently walked near him, then stopped, and leaned upon his rifle and watched the man at his work. For some moments he was unperceived, then, the fisherman looking up, with a terrified stare beheld the stranger, and, suddenly dropping the net, with a leap and a bound entered his hut, shut the door, and securely fastened it from within. Morgan was amused at the man's fright. He had evidently never seen a white man before, and although he tried to make him comprehend that no harm would be done him he was not able to make him understand a word.

The fisherman was watching the stranger from a crack in the wall of the hut when suddenly a large bird appeared above the tree-tops, flying around a circle as if in search of food. Morgan took aim at it and fired; the next minute the bird dropped at his feet. As it was not fit for food he left it lying where it fell. Finding all efforts to win the favor of the fisherman in vain, he went on the lower side of the house, where the nets were in the stream, and getting some nice large fish out of the net returned to his companions.

When he told them of the fisherman's fright they laughed heartily, and Kismut said, "I have heard of these fisherman; they live in a village several miles from my old home. They sometimes go far up in the jungle and set their nets for the fish in the solitary pools. That fisherman will leave the jungle immediately and will probably never return, for they are of the lowest caste, and are very superstitious."

Morgan now suggested that they have a good strengthening breakfast with the fish he had brought. Just then a troop of wild hogs rushed by them, and with quick aim he brought one down, and with his knife soon prepared some nice steaks. But Kismut shrank from eating flesh, or even eating with the others. It was violation of caste.

Morgan was surprised, for he could not comprehend the awful bondage of caste, but Nemorama, understanding it, patiently tried to overcome the widdow's scruple. She explained to her that, having placed themselves in the charge of the American, they were bound by his customs. She had no scruples, because she had never known the restrictions of caste and in this respect was on the same basis as their friend, while Kismut was now entirely without caste standing. She had left her home, had acknowledged herself to be as one dead, had taken a new name, had begun a new life, and had received the caresses of a "no caste" person, so that, while Mootie was indeed of high caste, Kismut was entirely without caste. She could not comprehend it. It was true she had no caste, and was Kismut, but she had Mootie's feelings, and the thought of caste violation horrified her. Never having eaten meat, she did not feel the need of it. Morgan patiently told them about the social customs in America, where there was no caste. All the people having the same rights, they talk freely together, ride in the same vehicles, eat at the same tables, and buy food from all classes of merchants. The only people who are disowned are the criminals, who are abhorred because of their vices.

When Kismut understood it she approved of it, and, although with some timidity, began to look upon her companions after the American custom, and for the first time in her life ate with those not of her caste; but Morgan alone ate of the steaks which Nemorama prepared for him. Then they proceeded together to the fisherman's hut, where they found Kismut's prediction verified. The fisherman had departed, and had taken with him all his nets and work-tools, also his sleeping mat and cooking utensils; a sure sign that he would not return. They were not sorry for this, as it furnished them with a house to dwell in until they should find a way to leave the jungle. After inspecting the house they went down to the stream just below it, and examined the fish-nets built in the water, which they found to be in good condition.

They were constructed in this way: "in a place where the water fell from a height the fishermen had dug out pits about the size of a house, and, laying them with stones in the form of the lower part of a cooking-furnace, they had heaped on stones above the pits, leaving only one passage for the water to descend; they had piled up the stones in such a manner that, except by this single passage, there was no other for the fish either to come or go. The water of the stream finding its way through these stones, this contrivance answered the purpose of a fish-pool. In winter, whenever fish were required, they opened one of these pits and took out forty or fifty fish at a time. In some convenient place of the pit an opening was formed, and, excepting at that outlet, all the sides of it were secured with rice straw, over which stones were piled up. At the opening was fastened a kind of wicker-work like a net; the two extremities being contracted were brought near each other. In the middle of this first wicker net was fixed another piece of wicker net-work in such a way that the mouth of this last might correspond with that of the other, but its whole length be only about half of that of the one first mentioned. The mouth of this inner net-work was made very narrow. Whatever entered passed of necessity into the larger wicker-net, the lower part of which was so constructed that no fish could escape back. The lower part of the mouth of the inner net-work was so formed that when fish had once entered the upper part they were forced to proceed one by one down to the lower part of its mouth. The sharpened sticks forming the lower part of the mouth were brought close together. Whatever passed this mouth came into the larger wicker-net, the lower passage of which was strongly secured, so that the fish could not escape; for if it happened to turn and attempt to swim back, it could not get up in consequence of the sharpened prongs that formed the lower mouth of the small inner wicker-net. Every time the fishermen bring their nets they fasten them on the water-course of the fish-pool and then take off the covering of the fish-pool, leaving all its sides secured by the rice straw. Whatever they can lay hold of in the hollow pit they seize, while every fish that attempts to escape by the only issue left necessarily comes into the wicker-net that has been mentioned, and is taken there." *

The fisherman had emptied the pools of their prey, but, in a few hours, more would be entrapped in them.

* *Memoirs of Mohammed Babur, Emperor of Hindustan.*

Seeing that the women were provided with a good, strong house for shelter and defense, and that an unlimited supply of fish was within their reach, and that they were happy in each other's company, Morgan decided to leave them to seek a way by which they might safely retreat from the jungle to some distant part of India. He knew the general course of the great highway running to the north, and going, as he supposed, toward it, reached it after several hours' vigorous traveling.

He had barely entered the travelers' bungalow when an attack of fever prostrated him, and the fear of death and anxiety for his wards caused him to rave in wild delirium. Fortunately he had with him some quinine, by the aid of which he was able to break the fever, and, though weak, in a couple of days was able to proceed with his plans.

Going to a village nearest to the highway he purchased three palanquins and hired coolies to carry them. Two of the palanquins were fitted up for the use of ladies, and he ordered complete suits, of such garments as high caste wealthy ladies were accustomed to wear when traveling, to be placed in them. With these he started on his return, anxious to find his charges in safety.

When the fisherman was sure that the strange being he had seen had returned into the jungle out of which he had come, he opened his door and cautiously picked up the huge bird so wonderfully slain. He turned it over and over until he saw where the bullet had entered on its fatal errand. Then, going down to his boat, he placed in it all of his movable property, all the fish in his nets, and last of all the bird, then swiftly pushed his way down the stream.

Hour after hour he steadily forced his boat ahead of the current, with the fear of that stranger continually in his mind. He could not think much, his mind was too dull for that, but he revolved over and over again every feature of the scene. It was no dream, no mere scare, for there was the dead bird before him. At length he reached the village, a cluster of low mud-huts, where his people lived, and in answer to their words of surprise at his early return he told them the story of the visit of the strange creature and showed them the bird he had slain.

While he was telling them about it, a holy fakir entered the street, and heard the story. Then he told the people of the strangers who had come to a village on the other side of the jungle and had slain the tigers. Perhaps this was one of them. Then seeing the bird he tore it open, and, finding the bullet, before any one noticed his action hid it in his hair. It was precisely the same as another bullet which he had already hidden there. Then he departed, while the people were bowing before him and begging for his blessing.

Just as the coolies were about to start with the palanquins engaged by the American the fakir arrived in their village. As he was passing the travelers' bungalow he noticed the American enter one of three carriages, the other two prepared for ladies, which were being taken into the jungle. A fiendish smile glowed on his wretched countenance; he felt sure he was now on the track of the missing maiden, and if his suspicions should prove correct he would be rewarded by a large sum of the rajah's gold.

CHAPTER XV.

JUNGLE EXPERIENCES.

WHEN Morgan departed from the fisherman's hut the women watched him until they could no longer catch a glimpse of his manly form. Then with arms intertwined they slowly returned to the open space on the bank of the stream, and ate of the berries growing there until they wished for no more. After this they proceeded to thoroughly cleanse the hut, and make it fit for them to dwell in. They laughingly talked of its bareness. The fisherman had been careful not to lose any of his property. He had not left a vessel to heat water or cook food in, nor a mat to sleep upon, nor a stool or bench; only the bare floor and walls of the hut. But this was far preferable to a cleft in the rocks or the branches of a tree. As they sat by the door of the hut their attention was attracted to a fierce-looking little animal that came out of the bushes and peered at them. Just then a bird also hopped upon the ground, when, quick as a flash of light, the animal pounced upon the bird, broke its head, and voraciously devoured it. Kismut said, "Ah! the fisherman had his pets. There is a mangouste, as savage as a tiger, but easily tamed by man. It has come to receive the caresses of its master. See, it is not pleased by our presence. How very quick and ferocious it is in attacking its prey. Let us look for its burrow; it must be quite near the hut."

The animal disappeared, and they looked for its retreat, but, not finding it, rambled along to the bank of the creek until they were near the place where they had first met each other. Here they sat down and talked about the past. Smiles illumined their faces as the sense of freedom and companionship filled their hearts. Solitary as their case seemed to be it was a delightful relief from the thralldom both had suffered but a few days before.

Kismut was enraptured with her new acquaintance. She had never before met any one like her, and the intelligence Nemorama displayed amazed her. Nemorama used freely words which Kismut had heard only from the lips of learned Brahmans, and even then spoken in tones of awful sanctity; names of the sacred persons and attributes, and of the relations of life. The freedom of utterance by her companion seemed as open and boundless as the jungle in which they were resting.

Kismut was a typical Hindu. She was almost perfect in simplicity and dependence. She had never learned any thing of the great outside world; her world had been the village in which she had always lived, and the surrounding jungle was the extreme limit of its attractiveness to her. The beyond was like a shadowy cloud—without form, and void.

Within her home it was entirely different. There she thoroughly understood all that was required of her. She had been a faithful wife, and her sun was her husband's smile, her shrine was at his feet. She had been taught this was right, and she never questioned this teaching. She was but a child in taste, and like all women of her class, this taste lay in the desire for ornaments. In all the misery of her lot nothing distressed her more than to be deprived of her ornaments. It was taking from her the only thing that could stimulate her to try and find pleasure or pleasant thoughts in a widow's life. In meeting Nemorama she met one whose life had been entirely different. Nemorama had worn so many ornaments that she was tired of the flashy baubles. Her taste was refined to desire only the more costly; such as very wealthy people wore—such as she saw decorating the peishwa and the ladies of his palace. She had met so many strangers, and had seen so many customs, that her vision of the great world beyond was that of a series of worlds, each one as great as India, and each one represented by these various people she saw coming to Bombay. She had been trained also in self-reliance.

In all her experience she had been compelled to depend on the skill of her own actions, the strength of her own muscles, and the retentive powers of her own mind. To possess this self-reliance she lost the confiding simplicity of her sisters, and she faced the world, not to be alarmed at its aggressive supremacy, but to conquer it.

Kismut had been religious in every thing, but Nemorama had not been religious in any thing. It was the death of Saineh that opened the torrents of religious conviction, along the currents of which the streams were still flowing. Kismut knew but little of the gods she worshiped. The idols were very mysterious to her. When she entered their presence it was to prostrate herself before them and worship, not to admire their forms. Nemorama knew stories about them all, and, with a desire to please, related the wonderful stories she had learned and had been accustomed to repeat before the select audiences in Bombay.

She repeated the tender passages from the Ramayana, and stories of gods and heroes, of battles and victories, until Kismut looked into her face with astonishment that any woman should know so much, and could so easily tell it to another. Then they talked about their hero, the noble stranger, who so tenderly and yet with such courtesy cared for them.

What a strange being he was; so different from any one they had ever known. They never saw him perform a religious ceremony, nor bow down to any thing in nature. He had no sacred trees, bushes, flowers, nor animals. To him they all seemed to be on an equality. Strangest of all was the indifference with which he ate his food. Fruits, leaves, vegetables, fish, birds, hogs, antelopes, and even buffaloes he partook of with equal relish, showing the most utter indifference to the prejudices of both Hindu and Mohammedan.

If a fly lighted upon his food, instead of cursing his companions and casting the food away, he brushed off the fly and ate the food. Instead of having his companions wait upon him, and eat what he left, he had them eat with him, and freely gave them the choicest parts.

And he had no respect for caste. He treated a coolie as deferentially as a Brahman, and only smiled when told that the Brahman sprang from the mouth of Brahma, and therefore is by right the chief of the whole creation, he alone having the right to the Vedas, to perform holy rites, to present ghee to the gods, and cakes of rice to the pitris. And, since the Sudra sprang from Brahma's foot, he should serve and honor the higher castes, and not make light of them.

Kismut said, "It must be his religion, for how can any one be without religion? and how can he be good except by the power of religion?"

Then Nemorama told her the story of Saineh. Drawing Kismut close to her, and caressing her fondly, she said: "You remind me so much of Saineh. My heart goes out to you as it did to her, and my heart is hungering for just such love as you can give. When I look into your eyes and read your growing affection for me, I see my Saineh over again, and I am glad." Kismut was overcome by this burst of affection, and she expressed her feelings by clasping her companion in her arms, and weeping upon her bosom. When Nemorama told the story of the death of Saineh and the comforting words of the missionary, Kismut asked, was not the missionary a believer in the same religion as their protector? Nemorama answered, "Yes; she, too, was an American. They both talked in the same way, and only last night in the tree he told me over and over the story of Jesus, whom he worships as God. Since then I worship him also."

"Tell it to me," Kismut pleadingly asked; and Nemorama, in low, sweet, tender words, told the story of Jesus as Morgan had given it to her.

Kismut listened with growing rapture. It was the sweetest and most hopeful story she had ever heard. It met the deep wants of her nature. And when Nemorama, with her own soul aglow, repeated the words of Jesus, "Come unto me, all ye that labor and are heavy laden, and I will give you rest. Take my yoke upon you, and learn of me: for I am meek and lowly of heart; and ye shall find rest unto your souls," Kismut felt the call as nothing had ever before affected her, and her soul was filled with joy. For awhile they sat in silence, thinking on this story of the Saviour of men; then as the shadows lengthened they watched the scenery about them.

They were in a great jungle; not that part which had once been in cultivation and had been allowed to grow rank and wild again, but where probably nature had always been in a wild state. Back of them rose a hill, covered with great trees—banyan, teak, ash, oak, pine, and others. In the thicker part of this grand forest the trunks of the trees rose to an immense height before the branches were stretched out, and the grove looked as though it had been growing for centuries. Below this grove and on the lower ground grew great tracts of bamboo—immense reeds, some many inches in diameter, and nearly fourscore feet in height. These grew so thickly that it seemed impossible for any animal to penetrate the area covered by them. Beyond this thicket the stream broadened into a marsh where grew a number of curious plants, one of which was the sola, the slender stems of which are used by the people of India to make artificial flowers and fancy ornaments with which they decorate their shrines at the Hindu festivals.

The women seeing some stalks of sola near by walked to the water's edge to gather them and exercise their skill in making ornaments while waiting the return of their friend. From this point they had a new view of the marsh, and to their dismay beheld a huge creature entering the marsh, puffing and snorting as he plunged into the water.

The animal was the dreaded rhinoceros. It was thicker than, though not so tall as, an elephant, but the horn upon its nose gave it an appearance of great ferocity. Their fears subsided as they remembered that, while the rhinoceros is very strong and ferocious when attacked, he is peaceable when left alone, and as he loved the marshes he would not be likely to come upon the higher ground where their hut was located. As they started to return they saw the convex flower clusters of the plant called mungoose, the plant that possesses the virtue of curing the bite of deadly serpents. Its presence suggested the presence of serpents, and the women walked with care lest they might tread upon one. As they quickened their pace they heard a great commotion among the trees. The branches seemed to be full of monkeys which were screaming and gesticulating in the greatest excitement; while upon the ground a large monkey was vainly struggling to free itself from the grasp of a huge serpent. The eyes of the serpent were like large balls of fire, while with wonderful celerity it wrapped its folds about the monkey, and in less than a second had crushed its victim into a lifeless pulp. The women were horror-stricken. They were so paralyzed with fear as to be unable to flee, and expected the reptile to attack them the next moment. Having crushed its victim, with anger unabated the serpent recoiled itself, hissed at the monkeys in the trees, and turned to lick its victim preparatory to swallowing it. But the hissing of the serpent had attracted the attention of a species of rat called mungoose, and a pair of them came out of the thicket and saw the serpent in its work. These rats have a deadly antipathy to serpents. They immediately rushed upon the monster, biting it, and causing it to leave its prey to defend itself.

The battle was a fierce one. The rats leaped about with astonishing celerity, while the serpent tried in vain to catch them in its folds. At length one of the rats fastened upon the serpent's head, and in a moment had penetrated the brain with its sharp teeth. With a strong convulsive movement the serpent tried to shake it off, then uncoiled itself and was dead. The other rat had been badly bitten by the serpent, and now that the battle was over ran down to the patch of plants called by the same name as itself, and vigorously began to chew both leaves and stem.

Recovering from their terror, the women hastened from the place, and did not cease running until they entered their protecting hut. The next day they only ventured out to obtain food, fearing that the companion of the serpent might be in the neighborhood seeking its mate. The following day, as they sat by the door of the hut, they heard the crack of a rifle, followed by a shout. Recognizing the voice of their friend they answered his signal, and withdrew into the hut. The coolies carrying the palanquins now brought them into the open place before the hut, and at Morgan's command withdrew to await his call.

Nemorama now came out of the hut and greeted her deliverer, then taking the contents of the palanquins again entered the hut. In a few moments she re-appeared leading Kismut, elaborately clothed in the garments provided for her.

Morgan gazed upon Kismut with admiration. Her face was wreathed in smiles of joy and affection, while a modest blush suffused her cheeks. Her saree was bound about her head so as to completely disguise her shaven crown. It was arranged in graceful folds about her waist, and falling down to her feet. Around her form was a tightly fitting blue silken bodice. Upon her neck, breast, arms, ankles, she had placed ornaments, while jewels sparkled here and there upon the gold-spangled saree.

As Morgan did not attempt to repress his admiration, she was filled with delight. The childish simplicity with which she displayed her gratification in the possession of ornaments only enhanced her beauty. Touched with sympathy, Nemorama folded her in a loving embrace and kissed her. Morgan now informed them of his plans, and, bidding them enter the palanquins, called the coolies, and they at once bade adieu to the jungle home, to return to the customs of civilized society.

No one saw a pair of eyes from beneath a mass of unkempt, mangy hair sharply staring at them as they passed a thick clump of bushes.

With silent tiger-like tread the fakir had followed the palanquins. He saw Nemorama greet the American. He knew by her dazzling beauty that she was the rajah's lost maiden. Slipping up to the palanquins, he put a mark upon them, and unseen regained his hiding-place. When Kismut came forth he was puzzled. In her new robes she was very beautiful. No one would have suspected her of being a widow. The fakir was puzzled. Who was she?

With fiendish delight he saw them depart. He thought they were in his power, and in due time he would not only solve the mystery of the second person but be able to deliver Nemorama to the rajah, and receive his coveted gold.

CHAPTER XVI.

FOES IN AGRA.

THE coolies bore their palanquins through the jungle speedily to gain the highway before nightfall. The fakir, familiar with the intricate paths, and sure of the success of his plan, took a shorter route, reaching the highway at a point several miles nearer the city to which they were going. Evening had fallen when Morgan reached the travelers' bungalow where preparations had been made for them to rest for the night. When he called the coolies to begin the journey next morning he found, to his surprise, that they had returned with the palanquins to their village, and another set of coolies, with palanquins of different pattern, were in their places. Asking why this change had been made, he was informed that a messenger had told the village chief that the American desired him to make such a change without delay, and, being paid for it, he had done so at once. Who the messenger was no one knew. If Morgan at that moment could have seen through the shroud in which a person near him was completely enveloped, he would have beheld a fakir of Hindu faith smiling with satisfaction at having circumvented the trick of a rival fakir of the Mohammedan faith. Seeing the marks upon the palanquins he had judged an evil design to be in it, and succeeded in having them changed.

Too late to redress the wrong, as he supposed it to be, Morgan gave the command to hasten. Past villages, fields of grain, forests of stately trees, swamps with miasmatic vapors, and jungles full of wild beasts and impenetrable by man, they hurried on their way. Past fakirs sitting by the road-side in the attitude of devotion, past streams of travelers, past lines of palanquins swiftly borne, past huge elephants and camels they sped, until they saw with satisfaction the red sandstone walls of Agra rising before them.

Agra, at one time, was the capital of the great Mogul Empire, and was located in the heart of the Mohammedan's vast dominion. In it was lavished the great wealth and the fine taste which marked the reign of the Moguls. Those old Saracens had been accustomed to dwell in tents, and when they settled in one place, and proceeded to build more substantial houses, they built after the patterns of their tents, substituting stone for canvas, and thus brought into existence an order of architecture peculiarly their own. They also built in strong contrasts. Red sandstone walls with white marble trimmings; swelling domes and slender minarets; heavy stone walls, massive and thick, with delicate leaf and flower carvings, and screens all carved in marble so thin as to let the light pass through the stone, and so delicate as to seem to be moved by the wind. Some of the buildings erected in Agra were unsurpassed anywhere in the world for combined beauty and strength.

The citadel, in which was the royal palace, was built on the bank of the river Jumna. Its wall was half a mile long and sixty feet high. It was built of red sandstone, while the pavilions of the palace were built of white marble.

Within this walled inclosure were handsome walks flowing fountains, flower-beds of rare beauty, and marble halls so arranged as to catch all the freshness in the air, keeping the place cool and enjoyable. The white marble pavilions were built upon a lofty terrace, and their domes were gilded so as to reflect with dazzling brightness the rays of the sun.

Along the walls were many little balconies, with delicate marble lace-work screens, like veils, hiding those inside from the gaze of those on the outside. Here the beautiful women of the Mogul court basked in a glory never excelled in material splendor, a glory which appears the richer to us through the subduing mists of antiquity.

The travelers hurried past this place, for the night was approaching, and the coolies did not vary the regularity of their tread until they came to the gate of the missionary compound. The coolies were now rewarded and dismissed. With their palanquins they proceeded to the resort of their people, to seek employment in carrying other travelers on the way toward their home.

Miss Thompson received the travelers with true Christian courtesy. Morgan had informed her through the mail service of their coming, and the manner in which he was seeking to save the women. She entered heartily into his plans, and when she saw them not only admired them for their beauty but loved them for their newly found faith. They needed her instruction, she was eager to bestow it, and they were ready to receive it.

Having seen them safely welcomed, Morgan departed to seek refreshment in the travelers' bungalow, rejoicing in the success which had thus far attended his efforts in their behalf.

The fakir who had crossed the jungle to intercept them safely and speedily reached the highway, and sitting by the road-side carefully scanned the palanquins that passed. Hour after hour he watched—all through the night, and the following day—but he did not see the marked carriages.

When he at length learned how his victims had escaped him his wrath was great. His thirst for revenge increased, and with haste he followed them to Agra.

Morgan considered himself fortunate in arriving at the old imperial city just when he did, for it was in the midst of extensive preparations to receive a rajah from the north with a gorgeous parade. For several days preceding, throngs of people from every direction came crowding into the city to witness the parades. Morgan was still more interested when he learned that the distinguished rajah was the one for whose harem Nemorama had been purchased. He had been informed of the tragic death of his dewan and the strange disappearance of the maiden, and had offered a large reward for the discovery of her fate. Thus far his reward had been unclaimed.

The parade of the rajah was the most brilliant display seen in Agra for many years. There were more than two hundred elephants in line, every one of them covered with splendid robes glittering with jewels. The officers of the rajah's court rode in the howdahs, and tried to surpass each other in the quality of the precious jewels sparkling upon them. Their howdahs, too, gave evidence of their wealth. Some were entirely covered with silver, some with handsome tiger skins, some were gilded with burnished gold—all were magnificent.

The servants of the rajah were numbered by the thousands, some on horses, some on camels, and multitudes on foot. Following the parade of the elephants came the household troops, marching with such uniformity and precision as to awaken the admiration of every one.

In the evening the city was illuminated, and the weird flashing of the lights added a thousand-fold beauty to the scene.

Morgan had never before seen any thing like it. It was in real life a scene out of the *Arabian Nights*

Entertainment. For a while he thoroughly enjoyed it, until he became aware of some one closely following him. Brave as he was he felt a chill of apprehension at the discovery. He was a stranger, without any particular means of protection, and alone. He reflected if his part in the events of the last few days should he be discovered what would be the revenge of the rajah and of the Brahman priests for his violation of their principles. In a few moments the dread passed from his mind as he looked at the marvelous display of fire-works closing the fête. Then, when all was over, with the crowds he turned toward the city to seek his resting-place. He had not gone far when a person completely shrouded touched him and requested him to follow.

Immediately he turned another way to escape the crowd. Although his guide, whether friend or enemy he could not tell, was just in front of him, he could not tell what kind of a man he could be, but he followed him in silence. By this time the moon was well up in the sky and casting a mellowing light over the earth, giving to every object a peculiar vividness, and to white objects startling prominence.

After a while they came to a lofty gate-way which he recognized. Passing through it they entered an avenue adorned with fountains and lined with cypresses. They walked along the avenue, until from amidst the branches of the trees Morgan beheld in dazzling whiteness, possessing an unearthly beauty from the playing of the beams of moonlight upon it, the Taj Mahal.

His guide led him to a seat by one of the fountains, where he could gaze upon the rounded domes, the slender minarets, and the massive walls so brilliantly white in the full rays of the moon, and set against the dark blue of the sky. Then his guide threw aside his shroud, revealing the hideous, filthy form of a Mohammedan fakir. So sudden was the change, so violent the contrast, that Morgan leaped from his seat and stared at him in speechless amazement. But the fakir calmly seated himself on the ground and motioning Morgan to resume his place, pointed toward the Taj and said, "American, do you see that wonderful building? I am told that there is nothing in the world to equal it. And yet it is in a country despised by your people as in gross darkness. You see its richness in jewels, its refinement of sculpturing, its elegance of design and perfect execution, and yet you boast of your mechanical and artistic skill, even while confessing you have neither the men to plan such a work, nor the workmen to execute it. You notice that its purpose is to honor a woman, and yet in your poverty and greed you boast how woman is honored in your land, and cry out against us because you say we despise women. Have you ever seen in your own land, or in any other land save this, any thing to honor woman as this does? Stranger, surely nowhere in the world is woman honored as she is with us. Do you not know that often-times our rulers have been entirely controlled by theirwives? Noor Jehan, the 'Light of the World,' was the real ruler of the empire, while all the ablest warriors of her time were compelled to honor her ability and power. Have you heard of Lakshmi Baiee, the queen of Jahnsee, who held the entire British army in check twenty-four hours, and would have come off victorious if a fatal bullet had not struck her down? Have you heard of Alleah Baiee, who for twenty years devoted herself to her people until all classes and all religions blessed her sweet influence? Or of Aus Khoor, who took charge of the disorganized State of Pattiala, and in one year restored order and established prosperity? Do you not know that in the popular stories taught the children of our country, the honor, bravery, and power of female heroes is loudly praised?

"In times of war our women have distinguished themselves as nurses, the equals of any in the world. In your travels have you not seen the richness of the houses of our princes, in which the finest verandas are for the women, in which they can recline upon the richest carpets of Persia, and enjoy an atmosphere laden with the choicest perfumes? Have you not read what one of our poets has written?

"'Her smiling countenance resplendent shines
With youth and loveliness; her lips disclose
Teeth white as jasmine blossoms; silky curls

> Luxuriant shade her cheeks; and every limb,
> Of slighest texture, moves with natural grace,
> Like moonbeams gliding through the yielding air.'

"You think you honor your women by parading them before the gaze and subjecting them to the remarks of all classes of men, but we honor woman by shielding her from this publicity. She shines within her own home. She cultivates a religious spirit, she studies faithfulness to her husband and children; she recognizes home as her sphere and contact with the world as the sphere of her husband. He is made strong to be able to cope with the temptations of the world. She is made tender and refined to grace with her loveliness the protected home, a place where she receives honor from all."

Morgan was again astonished. Another sharp contrast. Ideas in defense of purity and gentleness proceeding from the stained, coarse lips of a filthy, unwashed fakir. What would he hear next?

For a moment the eyes of the fakir were bent with almost a tiger's ferocity upon his own, and then the deep, harsh voice said, "Stranger, why have you come here to injure our women, and lead them astray? Is that the way you honor them? Why have you despoiled the house of the honored rajah by stealing his fair jewel, and hiding her from his loving search? Tell me! where have you hidden the nautchnee?

For a moment Morgan was alarmed. How came this man by his information? How much did he know? Recovering his tranquillity, determined to reveal nothing, he said with an air of calm indifference, as he returned the gaze of the fakir, "What did you ask?"

With eyes glittering like coals of fire, the fakir again asked, "Where have you hidden the nautchnee?"

With the same unruffled composure Morgan replied, "Who is she?"

The fakir then took two bullets out of his hair. Holding them up so that Morgan could see them he said, "With this one you pierced the heart of the bird; with it the rajah will pierce your heart. With this other one you pierced the brain of the elephant; with it the rajah will pierce your brain! Farewell."

Like a shadow he disappeared in the shrubbery and Morgan was left alone.

CHAPTER XVII.

THE SKIES BRIGHTEN.

As Morgan looked toward the Taj he became more tranquil. The tall slender minarets seemed to him as the white arms of women stretching heavenward in prayer, prayer for the deliverance from the bondage of caste and lust. There was absolute silence about him and he could think without interruption. He now realized his danger. The strange inscrutable power of the fakir was arrayed in deadly enmity against him, and his secrets were known. How they had been discovered he could not imagine, but there was the fact. They were known.

One thing was necessary to be done at once. He must get the women out of Agra, and out of his own company. If he must suffer the rajah's wrath, so be it, but if possible they must be saved. Somber reflections filled his mind as he slowly walked down the avenue, out of the gate, and along the deserted road to his bungalow.

Early next morning he went out upon the highway looking at the people as they carried on their ordinary avocations. As he recalled the splendid pageants of the day before he wondered what could check the power which these native chieftains exercised over the people. In a certain sense they honored the English, but they would not under any consideration eat at the same table with them, nor would they eat food upon which the shadow of a European had fallen, even though it be the queen's son. They were a subject people, but not in the least an affiliated people.

Looking toward the citadel Morgan saw the English flag waving, the emblem of the power which kept the land in peace. Seeing the flag, his courage was renewed, and he determined to pursue his course unto the end. Still, he did not see how he could claim protection, for was he not proceeding in violation of the customs of the land? Nay; he must work out the problem to the best of his skill, and if he failed he would fail like a man.

Snddenly his reflections were broken by hearing a familiar voice, and to the amusement of the people a big red-headed Irishman rushed up to him, and grasping his hand, while his eyes danced with delight, exclaimed, "An' sure, an' is it yerself, Mister Morgan, that I am seein, in this haythen place? By my troth it was reported of yez that yez had gone to make a supper for the wild beasts of the jungle, bad luck to them! Faix, an' I tole them as had the audacity to say the same that they didn't know the likes o' yez or they would niver make such a remark at all at all."

Morgan was heartily glad to see Dennis, and after

the first explosion of the Irishman's joy asked the welfare of Captain Grey. Dennis replied, "Sure, now, an' the captain is well, many thanks to yez, and is in his fortress among the mountains back of Bombay, an' he jest sent me up here to see if it was true as was reported of yez that yez was bein' after havin' died. An' now, bad luck to the loikes of thim as gave such reports to distress your friends, I can return and say the dead has come to life ag'in, an' the lost sheep isn't devoured by tigers at all at all. Beggin' your pardon, sur, but the captain will be mighty plased to know yez are a livin' bein', sur."

A plan now suggested itself to Morgan. Dennis was brave, loyal, and discreet; why not enlist his services to get out of his present difficulty? With a word of caution he led him out of the crowd, and out of the city; and when they were in the midst of a field, where no one could hear them, he told Dennis of his predicament, and the absolute need of outwitting the fakir, the rajah, and the host of their foes. Dennis was delighted with the romance of the situation, and vowed nothing would please him more than to take part in it, and promised even his life to his friend in order to save "the poor haythen craytures."

In a few words Morgan sketched his plan. Dennis's eyes opened wide with wonder at it, but he did not hesitate. By all the saints in his vocabulary he vowed he would faithfully carry out the part intrusted to him. Then they separated, each one to prepare for his part.

Morgan was hastening toward his bungalow when his attention was attracted to a crowd of people reverently bowing before a holy fakir. From the conduct of the people he imagined that this fakir must be of more than ordinary sanctity, for the women devoutly got down on their knees before him, and kissed the ground where his holy, unwashed and callous feet had trod.

Morgan drew near, impelled to study the man's manner of receiving these attentions and how he manifested the tokens of holiness. He first observed that it was a Hindu fakir, and the acts of reverence were from the Hindus. For a while he looked at him attentively, as the fakir sat motionless with closed eyes, more like a statue than a living person. After a while he opened his eyes and looked toward Morgan. In an instant there was a mutual recognition. It was the fakir who had committed to his care the nautchnee. Without a word, but by the changing expression of his eyes, he held the attention of the white man until the crowd had passed by and they were alone.

Then addressing Morgan by the word meaning foreigner, he said: "Feringhee, you have done well. You have shown that you possess a noble spirit. You have also learned what a treasure the maiden is whom I committed to your care. Do not be discouraged by the threats of your enemy, nor by the distresses into which you may fall. If you are wise and brave and true you will succeed in the end. Do not mind the way, keep the end in view. The enemy who led you to the Taj is still watching you, and has learned where the women are. You must remove them at once, but do not be seen with them in doing so. Send them to the south-west in the care of the Irishman. He will know how to protect them. Do not yourself go south until you see me again. I will find you. Beware of the Mohammedan fakirs. They are in the employ of the rajahs, and work for gold. If you need me, or are in trouble, find a Hindu fakir and show him this stone, and then I will come to you. Use this, however, only in an extremity."

With this he gave Morgan a brilliant ruby upon which were inscribed some mystical signs. The next moment he waved Morgan a farewell, as a crowd of people were approaching to pay him reverence.

That same evening, with cautious tread, as if unwilling to attract attention, Morgan took two palanquins, borne by coolies, to the missionary compound. They passed inside the inclosure, and after a short stay came out again and swiftly glided out upon the highway toward the east. As they did so the Mohammedan fakir sprang from behind a cluster of trees, and keeping in the shadows along the road, followed them. Morgan seemed to be urging the coolies to a more rapid gait than was usual with them, as they sped on toward Benares. When they came to their first resting-station, the fakir, watching his opportunity, again placed his mark upon the palanquins, and then leisurely went on in advance at a slower pace than they traveled. When after several hours he heard them coming he hid himself by the roadside, and soon had the satisfaction of seeing Morgan and his palanquins pass him on the road. Thus, with delight in his vigilance, the fakir followed them all the way to Benares.

The keen scent of the fakir was now matched against Yankee shrewdness. Morgan seemed to be exceedingly careful that no one should approach his palanquins. His coolies acted as if they were conveying most particular persons, of the highest caste, and while the curtains were kept so close that no one could possibly see the occupants with assiduous attention Morgan attended to their comfort.

While this scene was being enacted on the highway to Benares, another scene was being consummated in Agra. A short time after the departure of the palanquins from the missionary compound a lad left the gate and carefully searched the immediate neighborhood to see if any person was there in waiting. Seeing no one was near, he walked on his way toward the Taj. In a few moments another lad walked out of the gate, and proceeded in the same direction.

It was a beautiful night. The moon had risen and was casting its softened light upon the Taj, which was resplendent in all its wonderful impressive glory. There were crowds of people on the highway between Agra and the Taj—Mohammedans, Hindus, foreigners, travelers, pilgrims. It seemed as if all the world sent representatives to view the building on such charming nights. Palanquins were passing to and fro. Men on horses, camels, and on bullock-carts were hasting on their way. Merry parties with loud laughter or songs, others as silent as the moon in its march, some to wonder, some to worship—so the crowds moved on. The two lads joined each other on the way but were not distinguished as companions, because they spoke not, and others were pressing on by their side.

When they arrived at the beautiful tomb, accompanying a number of others, they followed a guide through the gardens, around the tomb, and then through its spacious precincts. Then having seen all the attractions of the place, they returned to the gate of the garden, and employed palanquins to convey them to the village leading into the country south of Agra.

By the Taj gate numbers of palanquins were in constant waiting for wearied visitors to the tomb, to convey them, for a small compensation, wherever they chose to go. The lads were taken to their destination, and at the travelers' bungalow called for a room in which they might spend the night. They dismissed their coolies, who returned to the Taj to serve other customers.

When morning dawned, they called for palanquins to convey them to the next village toward the south. Just as they were about to start another traveler, who had spent the previous day in the village, started in a palanquin going the same road. This last individual commanded the respect of all the servants about the bungalow. He was a tall, robust, dignified-looking man, clothed as a dragoon in the English service. With a free hand he paid his charges, and rewarded with extra sums those who diligently served him. He seemed to be very particular as to his palanquin and its furniture.

Seeing the others start at about the same time, he waited for them to precede him, saying loud enough for them to hear, "Whin I travel in a strange land like this I am excadenly careful of me kompany. An' 'tis myself would like to know if such as are in the pracading carriages are honorable and dacent, an' if so, thin I am plased."

The master of the bungalow informed him that the preceding company were harmless lads and he need not fear defilement from their touch or their words. Dennis then announced himself satisfied, and began his journey.

The lads seeing his red hair and hearing his broad brogue knew that he was their protector, and he knew that the palanquins before him contained Nemorama and Kismut, by the red ribbon which for a moment fluttered from the right hand window of their carriages. With swift pace and hopes of deliverance they passed on their way.

CHAPTER XVIII.

THE HOLY CITY OF THE HINDUS.

As Morgan drew near to Benares, he was compelled to proceed slowly, for the roads were crowded by the hosts of people flocking thither from all parts of the country, to be at the great mela just about to begin. The swarms of travelers pitched their tents in the open plains along the banks of the sacred Ganges, above the city. It was a curious spectacle made by the weary travelers as they reached the river and manifested the rapture of their souls by their leapings and prostrations. Some came on camels, some on horses, some on oxen or in ox-carts, but multitudes afoot. Mothers brought their little babes to wash them in the holy water. Old men and women with excessive weariness hobbled along to receive the blessing of a bath in the river. Many brought their aged, or their sick, to give them the blessed felicity of dying in sight of the sacred stream, while others eagerly welcomed any accident that might cause their death in so sacred a place.

In front of every tent fires were burning at which the women did the cooking for their households. Every one that came brought two baskets; one containing the food to eat, the other the ashes of their dead to cast into the flowing waters of the sacred stream. On the borders of the camp were the burning ghats, where those who died were consumed, and the ashes then flung into the sacred river.

All day long, and far into the night, the throngs crowded the banks, waiting their opportunity to enter the waters and bathe. It seemed to be a confused crowd of pilgrims, pressing upon each other, and yet they were most careful to preserve themselves from contact with those beneath them in caste. It was not now a question of wealth, culture, official favor, or meritorious distinction. It was caste, and even the distinctions of the remotest clanship within the general orders of caste were carefully sought for and acknowledged. The sacred cord across the breast was the symbol of power, and the pariah dared not so much as look into the face of a Brahman wearing the three-stranded cord.

The most superstitious ideas filled the minds of the pariahs concerning the power of these Brahmans to execute vengeance upon their enemies. The prospect of enduring the awful, unending, beastly or reptilian transmigrations for their disobedience or presumption was appalling to their stupid minds. The pariah, therefore, was as careful to keep out of the way of the white-robed Brahman as the Brahman was to avoid touching, even with the passing of his garments, the accursed pariah.

About two miles from the city, in an elegant

quarter, the English residents had built palatial houses with all modern improvements, and in a style of architecture combining the airiness desired in India with the solidity characteristic of their own land. Their suburb was, therefore, a constant reminder of their home land.

Morgan hastened to this place, and with a great show of style had the coolies convey the palanquins into private rooms, and after the distinguished ladies had alighted and passed into another room, the palanquins were removed. In this case the lady travelers happened to be bundles of old clothes. The coolies then bore their palanquins to the general rendezvous, while the fakir watched to see what would become of the ladies until the rajah's servants should secretly take possession of them. Benares was the holy city of the Hindus. To it they directed their pilgrimages, as the Mohammedans to Mecca, or the Jews to Jerusalem. It is the most ancient city in India, and from the earliest historic period has been the seat of Hindu learning and worship. It has more than three hundred mosques, with slender minarets pointing heavenward, in which the Mohammedans worship, and more than a thousand pagodas with lofty pinnacles sacred to the idols of the Hindus. Here is the great Sanskrit college of the Hindus, where their most brilliant scholars gather and study the Vedas. Here, too, Buddha preached his reform doctrines, and came so near to changing the religion of his people.

Here are located great manufactories, in which the greatest skill is displayed by Hindu workmen in their manufacture of silk, cotton, and woolen goods. In the bazaars of the city are to be found the finest shawls of the north, the diamonds of the south, and the muslins of the east. The city has more than two hundred thousand inhabitants, and this number is more than doubled during the melas, when the pilgrims come from all parts of the land. The city is built on the bank of the Ganges, the most sacred river in the world. The palaces of the wealthy crowd the river's brink for a distance of two miles; in some places so closely that the water has undermined the palaces, and the ruins show how powerfully at times the waters have swept along. Stone steps extend, the whole length of the city, to the water's edge, down which the people descend daily to bathe in the sacred waters. The Ganges is here about half a mile wide. All day long crowds of gaily ornamented boats glide on its surface. The city is built very compactly; the streets being narrow, and the houses lofty. The material used for building is mostly stone. In the streets of Benares, narrow as they are, the Hindus avoid, with the greatest care, touching, or being touched by, even the clothing of an unbeliever.

In the midst of such a population Paul Stanhope had set up the banner of the cross, and with all the fervor of his soul was telling the story of the love of Jesus. He did not have only poor, ignorant, heart-hungry people as hearers, but learned pundits, who were teachers of Hinduism, and skillful dialecticians from their schools, and sharp, disputatious, sophistical fakirs, and a people who, instead of hungering for the Gospel, were shocked at any intimation that their religion was not the best and the only true religion known to men.

With such audiences the difficulties of winning converts seemed to be almost insurmountable. The missionary was in his school-room, giving final instructions to his company of native helpers as to the places they were to occupy and the work they were to do during the days of the festival, when Morgan entered and beheld him for the first time since their parting in Bombay.

At the first glance Stanhope recognized his visitor, and with an exclamation of joy leaped from his chair, and with both hands extended in greeting came to meet him. His face, wreathed in smiles, told of the joy in his heart at seeing one of his own countrymen, and he said to Morgan, by way of explanation, "I never imagined how lonely one could be when week after week would pass by and only the faces of the people of other races meet your gaze. There are many compensations in a missionary's life, but the absence of one's own race is a hardship which grows upon you. We are constantly dealing with crowds. O what multitudes there are! and what a perpetual din of strange customs about us. Faces, faces every-where, until we look upon men almost as herds of cattle, and we yearn for the companionship of what seem to us to be real men—that is, our own English-speaking white-faced people. But now that you have come, I feel at home again.

"And you have been to Agra? Tell me all about what you saw there. Miss Thompson wrote me about your adventures, and she thinks you are quite a hero—in which opinion I coincide. But I cannot tell you how much I thank God that you are now a disciple of our Lord and Redeemer. I feel that you are a brother beloved in the Lord."

With this warm greeting Morgan felt an answering thrill of friendship, and at this moment, when heart beat in sympathy with heart, the missionary was dearer to him than any man had ever been. He, too, felt the sweet sensation of brotherly love, and joy filled his heart. His mind was full of questions. He felt that he knew so little of Christ, and now that he had opened his heart to the Saviour, he desired to closely study his word. Thus far he had an intellectual apprehension of the divine word; now he thirsted for the spiritual illumination.

When the two men were alone Paul Stanhope, with his Bible on his knees, in clear and logical order expounded to his friend the great doctrines of divine grace. Morgan spent the next day in watching the mela or religious festival of the Hindus. In various parts of the camp were the high poles, with flags flying from them, showing the location of the tents of those who had gottten up the festival. Around the edges of the camp were merchants with booths, selling every kind of an article the people would want either for use or ornament. In many places were pleasuring parties and dancing-girls to tempt and delude the unsteady. While the religious feature was most prominent, the attractiveness of sin and dissipation was not absent.

In some places throughout the camp learned pundits, or doctors of Hindu law, sat on the ground reading in a loud monotonous voice from the Vedas. Great crowds gathered around them to listen to the sacred words. In other places fakirs were sitting on the ground receiving the gifts and the adorations of the multitudes. Many of these fakirs were entirely nude, with filth like scales on their bodies, with their long hair, uncombed for years, matted together, and filled with filth. Their nails were untrimmed and resembled the claws of wild beasts. Many of them were the more hideous through bodily mutilations.

One had held his arm in an unchanged position for years until it could not be bent, and his finger-nails had grown down around his wrist. Another was reclining on a bed of sharp spikes that pierced his body whichever way he turned. Another had not eaten a morsel of food for a month, and did not intend to eat until the festival closed. Another had inserted steel wires into his flesh, and with a sort of fiendish delight

A GROUP OF FAKIRS.

was causing himself the most acute pain. Another had inserted hooks in his flesh beneath his shoulder-blades, and upon a high swing was swinging himself to and fro suspended by these hooks.

Before these fakirs the people gathered and prostrated themselves with greatest reverence. They awakened the most enthusiastic admiration, and the most hideous were the most admired. The pure-hearted, devout Hindu women with ardent devotion kissed the ground made sacred by the tread of these holy fakirs.

As Morgan watched them he learned another feature of fakir character—that was their intense jealousies. The various clans manifested this spirit, and the Mohammedan fakirs were in perpetual strife with the Hindu fakirs. Sometimes when they met they fought with each other, and in these contests displayed the ferocity of wild beasts. They knew no mercy, and only the death of one of them ended the struggle.

Their power of malediction was awful. They could utter the most terrifying imprecations upon their foes, and the fear of their curse was enough to make child, woman, man, or ruler offer great sacrifices to appease them. While this was the power of many there were others who were sincere devotees, who had given up the pleasures of life to become ascetics for God.

Some were learned Brahmans who were now fulfilling vows made, and they were honored with the greatest reverence because they had given up all the pride of life to become holy. The law giving directions to the sanynasi, or Brahman devotee—such as were some of these fakirs—for the thoughts he should cherish says: "A sannyasi should reflect on the transmigrations of men, which are caused by their sinful deeds; on their downfall into a region of darkness and their torments in the mansions of Yama; on their separation from those whom they love and their union with those whom they hate; on their strength being overpowered by old age and their bodies racked with disease; on their agonizing departure from this corporeal frame and their formation again in the womb; on the misery attached to embodied spirits from a violation of their duties and the imperishable bliss which attaches to embodied spirits who have abundantly performed every duty."

The moral courage of a life of such self-abnegation as was practiced by the truly devout fakir aroused the highest state of admiration and reverence in the hearts of the Hindus. To them a fakir was sacred. There were thousands of fakirs attending this mela, and in companies of hundreds they would march down to the river bank and receive the adoration of the passing multitudes.

As Morgan was observing one of these groups he saw the fakir who had led him to the Taj and had threatened him so furiously. As he looked at Morgan he máde a low and peculiar noise with his mouth.

Instantly every fakir in the company, following his gaze, looked at Morgan. For a moment Morgan's heart felt faint, for he knew that from this moment he was a marked man, and that every one of these fakirs would seek his destruction. He hastily passed to another part of the camp. As he passed by another group he beheld the fakir who had befriended him, and when he saw the large company of Hindu fakirs surrounding him he felt assured that he would find help in the time of need. He continued on his way until he came once more to the missionaries' tent.

The missionaries' tent was established by the side of the main road along which the crowd must pass to get to the river. The missionary, assisted by a number of native helpers, was spending his entire time in preaching, tract distributing, and selling Bibles and various religious books.

Paul Stanhope had carefully studied the Hindustance language and the dialect in most common use about Benares, and was able to address the people in their own tongue. As he preached to them some laughed at his words, some listened with deep interest, and some kept up a running comment upon his statements or asked him questions.

At times it seemed to approach a free debate, in which there would be sharp questions and sharp answers. Now a Hindu pundit would interpose a question, now a Mohammedan moulvie would deny his statements, now a fakir would resent his teachings, now a passing show of actors or curiosities would break upon his audience—and so the work went on. The crowds were always ready to enjoy his defeat if they got such a chance, or to laugh at his victory if won by smartness. The quickness of the Hindu's mind in suggesting illustrations and analogies was wonderful, and the missionary soon learned that in the crowds before him were men of great learning, knowing well their sacred books, and able debaters of their faith. When he became convinced that these public discussions only amused the people and did not convert them, he turned from that method and preached the simple story of the cross.

To this the people listened; to know more of it they read the tracts and purchased the books, and when daylight had passed many of them came to the missionary tent to inquire more particularly into these things.

In this manner the work was carried on day after day, and the story of Jesus was taken by these pilgrims to their distant homes. The missionary received many invitations to visit their villages and preach more of the glad tidings of forgiveness and salvation to them. It was so different from the religions they had known, and it was as a refreshing fountain to their thirsting souls.

The missionary noticed that, as a rule, those who received his doctrine were the low caste people, or the pariahs, and only occasionally a Brahman. The multitudes of high caste people, clothed in pure white robes, passed him by without deigning to heed his call.

The unceasing nature of the work, from the break of dawn until late at night, was a great strain upon his nerves, and long before the feast closed his strength began to give way. It seemed as if years of labor must be crowded into one month. He kept to his post until the close of the feast, and then, utterly prostrated by his toil, hoped for rest.

CHAPTER XIX.

DENNIS IN TROUBLE.

DENNIS took charge of the ladies with the firm resolve to break the head of any man that attempted to interfere with them or hinder their journey. His honor was at stake. A trust had been laid upon him which he considered sacred. His heart swelled with pride as he thought of his unique position in the midst of a stealthy and heathen people. His courtesy could not be excelled. At times in the course of the journey he surprised the ladies by the manner in which he would assure them that they could fully trust him.

They had resumed their female attire with the second change of coolies, and he had taken the charge of the three palanquins. They readily perceived that he was showing them loyal gallantry, but it was in a manner just the opposite of that to which they were accustomed. They were quiet, he was noisy; they uttered but few words, he was talking all the time; they interspersed many religious observances in their daily life and conversation, he seemed to be utterly without such. But they were satisfied, because they had complete trust in the judgment of their protector and in his assurance that Dennis was honest, loyal, and brave.

Impressed by the warnings he had received, Dennis was constantly observant of fakirs. Numbers of them were passed on the road, for they abounded in India. It was popular to be a fakir. He had often heard Captain Grey tell how they carried the secret messages of the rajahs which caused the surprise in the mutiny of 1857; and whenever he saw one he thought some secret must lie hidden in his mind, to some day be given out in the cause of evil. He was just a little afraid of their treachery. It would have afforded him great pleasure to have broken some of their heads with his club, but he well knew that if he raised his hand against one of them the fanaticism of the people would be aroused and every man would hasten to resent the blow.

Dennis delighted in military regularity; and as he watched how gracefully the coolies carried the palanquins hour after hour, he was loud in his praise of their service. At the end of the third day's journey, as they alighted for rest from the palanquins and entered the travelers' bungalow, Dennis noticed the sharp eyes of a fakir observing every motion, and he knew that they were being watched. At the close of the next day the same thing was repeated. This time the fakir did not make himself prominent. His manner would have indicated to a stranger utter indifference to what was passing about him. But Dennis saw behind this outward show. The keen glitter and subtle expression of the fakir's eyes could not be misunderstood. Dennis assumed an air of unconcern before others and seemed to be in a happy mood, but not a word escaped him regarding his companions or the object of their journey. But when alone in his palanquin his brow was wrinkled in deep perplexity, and he frequently shook his head and muttered to himself as he sought to solve the problem how to elude his pursuers.

After a while he observed that different fakirs were watching him, and he began to comprehend the system of telegraphing by which they girdled India. He saw that they did not work as solitary individuals, but as an organized band, and his fear of them increased. Whenever he came in sight of the flag of England his courage revived and his heart grew light, for he feared no treachery beneath its folds; but sometimes days passed in which he seemed to be in the heart of heathenism. Dark faces, primitive social customs, multitudes of people, towns with many pagodas, troops of fakirs, and wretchedness crowded the country through which they were passing. They also frequently passed through patches of jungle in which man-eating tigers had their lairs and deadly serpents crawled. Through such places they hastened in silence and in fear, and they never entered them near the hours of darkness.

They were passing through one of these lonely and long stretches of jungle, when a number of men suddenly sprang out of the bushes and with savage shouts rushed upon them. In an instant Dennis leaped from his palanquin to the ground and commanded the coolies bearing the maidens to go on. As the brigands endeavored to stop the coolies, Dennis drew his revolver and shot the man who had laid his hand upon the foremost palanquin. The man fell, but another sprang to take his place. Dennis quickly shot him also; and as he fell the palanquin was liberated, and the coolies bearing it rushed down the road with all the speed they possessed.

The brigands now closed about the other palanquin, and the coolies, thoroughly frightened, dropped it and ran for their lives. Dennis stood by it and fought the robbers, every shot of his revolver with unerring aim felling a foe. But the barrels were soon empty, and the crowd of foes pressed upon him so fiercely that he could no longer defend himself and fell to the ground beneath their clubs, bleeding and senseless. The brigands, supposing him to be dead, left him with their slain comrades and hastily retreated into the jungle, carrying the palanquins which the coolies had forsaken.

Dennis was blessed with a thick skull, and in a short time regained the use of his senses and beheld the carnage about him. His first thought was, "Where are the ladies?" Those committed to his care were taken from him, and he was still alive. What would he say to Mr. Morgan, to Captain Grey? His head was racking with pain, but this thought was torture to his heart. He would rather have been killed in the battle than live with this disgrace. He sat down, and pressing his head between his hands looked at the evidences of the struggle. By his side were the robbers he had slain. He counted them. Every bullet in his revolver had cost a man his life. For a moment he was silent, and then he arose and exhausted his vocabulary in maledictions on his foes. The shadows were lengthening, and with the darkness hyenas or wolves would come out of the jungle and so completely devour the slain that by the morning's light not a trace would be left of them. Fearing he might suffer the same fate, he took one of the brigands' clubs in his hand, and with his empty revolver in the other hand, walked back to the village through which he had passed only a couple of hours before.

Dennis had learned something of the political system of the provinces in India, a system of village government as old as the Aryan invasion.

The unit of government in India is the village, and each villag e community is a little republic having every thing within itself, and in the most of cases entirely independent of foreign relations.

The holders of land, farmers, mechanics, and workers of every kind, compose the commune, sustaining a relation toward each other like the members of a family to one another. Their code of morals is determined largely by this relation. They are truthful, honest, and accommodating to each other, while to foreigners, or the people of some other village, they may present an entirely different character without thinking it to be wrong. To lie to one of their own village would be a disgraceful act, but to lie to one of another villlage would be shrewdness, and not wrong-doing. This code of morals they observe in all the acts of life. It shows the narrowness of heathenism; all the world outside the borders of their own village being considered legitimate ground for preying.

When we remember that India has 448,320 villages with less than one thousand inhabitants each, we can see why they have been so easily conquered by the English, and why they are held in restraint when there is only one Englishman to every thirty-five hundred of the people of India. Their villages, as a country, have no cohesive attraction. And yet there is a sort of a union. Sometimes a number of villages will unite in a confederacy which they call a *gramagala.* There is also a system of taxation by which one officer will collect taxes from many villages for the one who holds the land in subjection. When eighty-four villages are united for this purpose, it is called *katurasite.*

Dennis had been assailed within the borders of one of these villages, and knowing he could hold the village responsible for his loss he determined to enforce his claim for justice and reparation.

When he reached the village he sought the dwelling

of the chief man, and while a crowd gathered about him, loudly complained of the injuries he had received. They could not deny his having passed through their village so recently, and his bruised and bleeding face was evidence of the blows he had received. Alarmed at the serious aspect of the affair, the chief man immediately dispatched a number of men to the scene of the conflict, to be witnesses of the harm done. When these men arrived at the place they found the hyenas fighting over the bodies of the slain. Driving them off with their torches, they examined the bodies, and pronounced them to belong to a band of robbers whose stronghold was in the jungle, and that for a long time they had been molesting travelers. Notwithstanding the gusto with which this information was given, Dennis was not disposed to accept it as a final settlement of the affair. What he wanted was his palanquins and the companions of his journey. With thorough Irish vehemence he boasted of his being an officer of the government, on important business with distinguished companions, and if the villagers did not make the matter right the government would.

The violence of manner with which Dennis made this threat thoroughly frightened the villagers, and they promised to collect at once a strong body of men, and, as soon as daylight came, to do all they could to discover the stolen persons and property.

While gathering the men for this mission, torches were seen rapidly approaching on the highway.

When they came near, they were seen to be torches borne by the coolies who were the bearers of the palanquins in which the nautchnee had been traveling, who had escaped the robbers by rushing forward in obedience to Dennis's command. When they arrived at the next stopping-place, they discovered that their passenger had mysteriously disappeared, and they immediately returned in search of her. Dennis examined the palanquin. Nemorama's garments and possessions were there, but she was not, and there were no signs of a struggle or confusion in the palanquin.

He was now more distressed than ever. The villagers could not restrain their pity as they witnessed his deep anguish of spirit. Physical exhaustion and the excessive pain from the wounds he had received rendered him incapable of controlling his emotions as he thought of the probable fate of his wards.

Soon after daylight the villagers were ready to start, and a large number of excited men followed Dennis and the village chief to the place of the conflict. Scouts were sent out who soon discovered the trail of the brigands, and with rising enthusiasm the entire party plunged into the jungle.

For a long distance their track was in a forest of lofty trees, which they pursued until they came to a ravine in which a flowing stream hid all traces of the brigands from their sight. The scouts scoured the ravine, but were utterly unable to discover further signs of the trail. In doubt and perplexity they continued down the ravine until they came to a place where great masses of rock shut in the stream, showing the possibilities of an ambuscade by which they might all be slaughtered. As they stopped to consider what course to pursue, their attention was attracted to a person climbing down the rocks toward them, and evidently anxious to reach them. As the person came nearer, Dennis was enraptured to see that it was Nemorama. Her garments were badly torn, and she was suffering from fatigue, her feet were bleeding from the cuts and bruises inflicted by the sharp stones over which she had passed. She was so eager to tell her story to Dennis that she seemed unaware of the presence of the others. She said: "When I was borne away from the conflict, I knew from the numbers of assailants that they would conquer. When at a safe distance the coolies stopped for a few moments, and ran back to see how the battle was going; then I slipped out of the palanquin, closed the curtains, and hid myself in the bushes. The coolies returned quickly, and were too excited to notice the lightness of the palanquin, but with rapid strides pressed on their way. I cautiously returned to the place of the conflict, and seeing the robbers carrying Kismut with them, followed them, hoping by some chance or other to be able to deliver her. O, it was hard work to perform. The robbers traveled rapidly, shouting and cursing as they went, and I following, in fear lest I might lose them, or they might discover me. When it became dark they had their torches, but I could only follow their lights. Many times I stumbled and fell, then I was in fear lest the breaking of a twig, or a stone falling down the hillside, moved by my tread, might attract their notice. The thought of venemous serpents in my way also came into my mind, and only the hope of delivering Kismut gave me strength to continue. When they came to these rocks, they ceased their shoutings, and slowly climbed them, and then proceeding along a very dangerous way, came to their den, and there Kismut is now in their grasp, and they are resting until it suits them to go on another foray."

The men were now anxious to proceed, and as Nemorama pointed out the way they moved forward as silently as it was possible for them to tread. Above the rocks, the narrow path ran by the side of great ledges, by deep precipices, and around sharply jutting crags. Dennis noticed that in such a place a few men could keep at bay great hosts, but the robbers thoughtlessly left the pathway unguarded. After a while they came to a plateau, and saw before them the robbers' resort. It was a cave in the side of a great mass of rocks. Before the cave was a level area upon which the robbers were taking their ease. Some were lying asleep, some were chatting with companions, some were eating, while others seemed to be discussing plans for future deeds.

Their resort was in the depths of the jungle. The jungle for many miles lay below them, and off in the distance the highway, like a slender thread, was seen. It was a fortress and a watch-tower, and as Dennis marked its features as a fortification he did not wonder that the robbers had never been overcome.

Dennis now quietly communicated to his followers his plan of attack, and then, with a rush and a yell, they all sprang forward, and before the robbers could recover from their surprise were upon them. The conflict was short and desperate. The surprise was complete, and in a few moments all the robbers who were not killed or badly wounded had fled down the narrow path beyond their cave.

Going into the cave they found the palanquin, and Kismut in it suffering from the terror which the menaces of the robbers had produced. Folded in Nemorama's arms she soon recovered tranquillity, and then the entire party prepared to return to the village. The cave was well stocked with provisions and weapons, and in it were also found great stores of goods stolen from defenseless travelers. The chief villager had an account taken of all the possessions found in the cave, and, with the wounded robbers as prisoners, began the homeward march. The women were gently borne in the palanquins, and Dennis was carried in a palanquin hastily prepared for the purpose. Now that his wards were recovered he showed utter prostration, and as he was being carried slept so soundly that the village was reached before he awoke.

On the following day, having recovered from his fatigue and his wounds having been bound up with ointments, he resumed his journey, anxious to reach Bombay before the beginning of the inclement season.

CHAPTER XX.

ZENANA WORK OPENED.

IN a village not very far from Benares one of the missionaries had established himself, and was building up an extensive work. He chose the village in order to be away from the curious crowds of the city, where he could preach and teach those who in quiet desired to learn. When the mela was over he insisted that Stanhope should come to his home and rest. Morgan encouraged his friend to do so, and promised, as an inducement, to accompany him.

It was an ordinary village. The houses were constructed of bamboo frame-work covered with matting or with mud, with a thatched roof extending over it all. These houses, simple in construction, were built very light, and closely along narrow lanes. Most of them contained large families, often several generations dwelling in the one house.

Generally when a fire broke out in one of these houses it swept the street and caused loss of life, for the flames spread so rapidly that it was impossible to extinguish them. This, however, was but seldom, because the religious customs of the people led them to exercise great care in all they did. In front of most of the houses the plant called mehndee was cultivated. When in blossom it is very pretty with its small, delicate, fragrant flowers resembling the clematis.

The high caste Hindu women cultivate this plant to afford them dyeing material. They bruise the leaves, and then moisten them with lime-water. They then apply this mixture to their nails, tips of the fingers, palms of the hands, and often the soles of the feet, which in a short time become a reddish-orange color, the stain remaining until the skin is worn away. In these villages the people are very particular in presenting their caste and clan symbols.

"The sectarian marks of the Hindus vary with their caste and the deity to whom they attach themselves. The high caste Brahman makes only a circular mark with a little sacred mud of the Ganges, mixed with water, on his forehead. This is symbolic of the mystic word '*Aum.*' The followers of Vishnu, a second grade of Brahmans, use a species of clay brought from a pool, Dhwaiaka, in which the seven shepherdesses who are always represented with Krishna are supposed to have drowned themselves on hearing of the death of their favorite hero. This mark is a circle with a straight line passing through, symbolizing the regenerative powers of nature. The Mahadeo sect wear two straight lines on the brow; the one on the right stands for God, the one on the left for man. A transverse streak of red lime (a preparation of turmeric and lime) joins them, signifying God and man united. A great many wear the mark of Vishnu's weapon with which he is supposed to have killed the sea monster to rescue from destruction the three Vedas. The followers of Siva, one of the four great sects of Hindus, wear a complex mark of circle and cross combined, made with the ashes of burnt cow ordure, symbolizing the destrnction of all sin and the beatitude in store for the pure and holy."

Thus every man carried his mark, which at a glance manifested just what belief he held. No Hindu was ashamed of his religion.

In the villages each sect had its own pagoda, to which the people freely gave their offerings. They always took an offering when they approached their god.

The missionary built his station, or compound, on the outskirts of the village, on a piece of elevated ground by the side of the main road, and in a place with abundant shade.

The main building, or missionary bungalow, was a large one-story house, built of bamboo and mud, and kept attractive with whitewash. The thatched roof extended over the verandas, under which the air circulated through wide doors and windows.

The chapel was built of the same material. In htis building morning and evening prayers were offered, and on Sundays the people were gathered for more elaborate instruction. The school-house was open six days of the week, and closed on Sunday. Here various branches of learning were taught, and all the boys and girls of the village were welcomed.

There was one more building in the compound, called the orphanage, where waifs were gathered. Some of these had been deserted by their parents—poor little girls, who found no welcome in a community where there were already more girls than boys. Some of the children had lost their parents by that dreadful scourge of India—the cholera. Having no friends to care for them, the missionary took them in. These children were all being trained to become heralds of salvation. Hinduism built asylums for monkeys, decrepit elephants, bullocks, birds, and even reptiles, but Christianity built asylums for children. By kindness, counsel, and free instruction the missionary gradually won the regard of the people, and his work flourished. Here, in the midst of Hinduism, he had set up as an example and pattern for the people a typical American home.

It was a matter of curiosity not only to the people of that village, but to the people of the surrounding villages, and to the visitors and pilgrims who passed along this road going to the sacred Ganges. As they looked into it they observed the liberty, happiness, and comfort of a Christian home. To this comfortable place Paul Stanhope came, and rested his wearied body beneath the shelter of the wide verandas, occasionally speaking words of exhortation or counsel in the chapel or school-room.

For a few days the change seemed to benefit him. then came a turn for the worse, and with sorrow his friends perceived that his days on earth would be few.

As Stanhope saw the anxiety in their faces, he easily guessed the cause, and with calm patience gave himself up to the will of God. The only desire he seemed to have was to see Jennie Thompson before he died. He had no sooner expressed this desire than Morgan started for Agra to bring her to him.

Jennie Thompson's work in Agra had been constantly increasing. As the people learned to know her gentleness, and that love for them had caused her to come among them, they watched for opportunities to hear her sweet voice, or to feel her gentle touch. They had been accustomed to hear their pundits reading their sacred books in drawling tones, but the reading of the Gospel to them in expressive tones, slowly enough for them to understand, and illustrated from their own customs to make it plain, opened their hearts so that the more of it they heard, the more they desired to hear. But her work was not in the missionary bungalow, it was zenana work. She represented the work of the women of America for the women of India. She did not wait for the people to come to her, she went to them to bless them, to carry to them a bright and cheering light. In the houses of the wealthy the zenanas were furnished with many comforts. They were airy and light, with beautiful and fragrant gardens before the verandas, with high walls surrounding the gardens. But with the poor there were no such comforts. Their rooms were dark, gloomy, and devoid of every thing that could make life sweet and cheerful; and the most of the people were poor. Yet, whether in the houses of the rich or poor, there was a kind of seclusion insisted upon that shut these women in from sympathy or participation with the life of others. The men, the little children, and dissolute characters had the freedom of the street. Such was the peculiar nature of Hindu social life.

The wretchedness of the women in poor families awoke the most tender feelings in the heart of the missionary. She saw her sisters in the bondage of social and religious customs which were blighting their lives and rendering them incapable of exhibiting those features of feminine grace and usefulness so common in her own land. In the houses of the wealthy she saw that, with all the advantages of wealth, their lives were spent in idleness and gossip, in self-decoration and frivolity, while the nobler parts of their nature were entirely neglected. To such she desired to show how useful they might become, and by helping those in suffering they might obtain the most enduring rewards for their own lives. At first the doors of these houses were closed against her. The people had nothing in common with her. She was a foreigner, representing a strange and antagonistic religion. She was defiled by her habits, by the food she ate, the company she kept, the things in life about her that touched her. She made companions and disciples of low caste, of pariahs, and of people below caste. Her very touch would be pollution.

But after a while they began to listen to the accounts of her success in healing diseases. The poor fever-stricken woman whom she healed loudly spoke her praises. The woman who for many years had been unable to leave her bed, and through her treatment was now able to walk as freely as ever, went from house to house telling the story of her wonderful cure. By-and-by she acquired fame, and then the Hindu physicians, soothsayers, priests, and astrologers began to upbraid the people for having any thing to do with her, for they saw that she was taking from them their influence and their fees. The turning-point in her usefulness came as a result of a man's strong affection for his wife.

The wife of a prominent high caste man was lying very sick. With all his love for her he was not willing that a man, even though a physician, should enter his zenana. Hearing of the success of the strange woman he sent for her, and, charmed by the grace of her speech, the courtesy of her deportment, and the beauty of her countenance, opened the hitherto closed doors.

The beautiful wife had been ailing for a long time, and was now unable to leave her couch. Her husband lavished upon her all the attentions she could desire. He spared no expense to benefit her, but all in vain. When Miss Thompson entered the zenana she was greeted with looks expressive of great anxiety from the invalid and her attendants. She breathed a prayer to God for his blessing and that he would grant her this soul. Then she carefully examined the invalid. When the examination was completed the name of a peculiar and rare remedy flashed into her mind, and believing it to be from God she began to administer it to the invalid. All that day she remained in the zenana, and the next day, and the day following; then, seeing the patient on the road to recovery, she departed amid the thanks and rejoicings of all.

From this she was called into other zenanas until she had established many firm friendships among the high caste ladies. At first when with them she said nothing about her religion except to answer their questions, but afterward she read to them out of her Bible the sweet stories in the gospels of Jesus going about doing good. In this way she brought the light and power of the truth to bear upon many hearts, until they too rejoiced in Christ as their Saviour. As a physician her heart often felt sad as she saw how much her sex suffered from the ignorance and wrong treatment of the Hindu physicians.

Many suffered for years who might have enjoyed good health through a little proper treatment. Wretchedness, pain, and misery became their punishment for wrong social views, and she determined to see what her influence could accomplish in teaching her sex the rights that belonged to them by the nature God had given them. She taught them to have more light, and to drive darkness and gloom out of their dwellings. They should have plenty of pure air and not be shut in stifling rooms. She also urged them to employment, and to resist the temptation to be idle. They should always have something to do. This would add to their cheerfulness. She also urged them to obtain knowledge.

This was a decided innovation which they did not dare to indorse. This was the privilege of the men, not of the women. But in the missionary school all who accepted Christ were taught to read. It was necessary that every one should read for herself the word of God. Christianity and intelligence went hand in hand. Purity of heart and strength of mind were sisters.

Thus her work moved on. As she read Paul Stanhope's letters she grew sad. Was he indeed so sick a man? When Morgan came for her, she laid down her work to go to her heart's beloved, and as Morgan watched her countenance he saw that her heart was battling with the sorest trial of her life.

A MISSION STATION.

CHAPTER XXI.

THE MISSIONARY'S REST.

WHEN Morgan and his companion reached the compound, Stanhope was reclining in an easy-chair on the veranda watching for them.

Miss Thompson was hardly prepared for the decline of vitality which she saw, and it required all her force of will to keep back the tears. Stanhope received her with joy. His eyes were full of hungry yearning. Smiles covered his face, but as they quickly fled away, the hollowness of his cheeks was the more plainly revealed. He took her hand within his own, and feasted his eyes upon her countenance, listening with calm delight to the melody of her voice as she told of her success in zenana work in Agra. Then, wearied with excess of joy, he went to sleep in his chair, still lovingly clasping her hand.

When night came and she retired to her room, the flood-gates of her grief were opened, and she wept with such anguish of soul as she had never known before. She was oppressed with a sense of her loneliness. For a moment a wave of homesickness rushed across her heart, and she thought, "O mother! mother! If I could only weep on your loving bosom in this hour of my sorrow!"

Then she thought of her mission and of his mission. He so noble, so intellectual, a man of moral grandeur, a man to sway thousands, now dying at the threshold of usefulness. Was this God's way? As she thought of heaven she became calmer. It would be more real to her when he should enter its pearly gates, and he would be nearer to her than ever before. All night long she fought the battle with her sorrow, but by the morning's light she rejoiced in having gained the victory, and could say, "My soul is resting in peace."

As Morgan saw his friend growing weaker, an intense desire sprang up within him to prolong that life if possible. India was favored with many health resorts. The magnificent mountains bounding the peninsula on the north were intersected by many charming little valleys at the head-waters of great rivers stretching clear up into the regions of eternal snow. All degrees of climate could be found, and sanitariums adapted to all kinds of invalids. Perhaps some spot might be found to benefit Stanhope and rob death of its victim.

Expense was no consideration. He consulted his friends, studied maps of the country, searched the guide-books, and then, having decided upon the place, astonished Stanhope and Miss Thompson by bidding them prepare for an immediate journey to Nynee Tal.

Palanquins were soon in readiness, and Morgan, with Stanhope and Miss Thompson, were on their way. They were carried to Benares, where they entered the cars and rode through Lucknow to a point on the railroad nearest their destination. There *jampans* were provided, and the march up the mountain was begun. Jampans were arm-chairs with a pole on each side, and carried by four men. The path up the mountain reminded Morgan very much of traveling in Switzerland. The narrow road wound around one peak after another of the mountain, sometimes between high rocks and yawning precipices, sometimes in places where it seemed almost a puff of wind might cause devastating land-slides. As they passed along the cold increased, and the shrubbery on the mountain indicated the change in the climate. The cool air seemed to nerve them all, and the invalid almost forgot his weakness in beholding the grand scenery stretching out below their path. Before the journey was ended he gave way to fatigue, and as the coolies tenderly bore him along he restfully slept. At length they reached Nynee Tal, and were soon placed in comfort in a large sanitarium provided for the accommodation of guests.

Nynee Tal is in a narrow valley between two spurs of the Gaghur range of mountains. It is seven thousand feet above the plain, and is just in front of a mountain range twenty-one thousand feet higher, and covered with perpetual snow and glaciers.

The valley is half land and half water. The water, being at all times transparent and like a mirror, reflects the surrounding mountains. It is one oft he most charming spots in India, and if Paul Stanhope's life could be saved, this was the place to accomplish it. It had been used as a sanitarium so many years that all the conveniences for an invalid's comfort were at hand, and Morgan gave explicit instructions that nothing should be spared that might assist the invalid in his search for health.

There were many English residents in the place and health-seekers from all over India, and travelers from all parts of the world seeking temporary rest in their journeyings. With nothing to weary him and every thing to interest him, Stanhope gained strength for a time, but Miss Thompson was not deceived by these appearances. She knew that soon and suddenly an attack would come which would probably be fatal, but with all her skill and affection she watched his symptoms and guarded him from every aggravating cause. As she watched over him, read to him, and in a thousand little ways displayed her affection for him, she manifested a sweetness of disposition that led the people to speak of her as an angel ministrant.

As he drew nearer the end of life she experienced a strong desire to bear his name. According to the custom of India she would be his widow if he died, but not according to the custom of her home-land, and she wished to be recognized as his own to her own people. He, too, was desirous of calling her his wife, if only for a day. He could not dismiss from his mind the idea of many in India that she would be his, if true, for all eternity. The ceremony was not delayed. Invitations were sent to all the Americans who were visiting the place and to all the guests of the sanitarium.

They gathered in the large dining-hall, and when they had taken their places the Hindus and native Christians and servants crowded upon the verandas and into the unreserved parts of the room, all curious to witness a marriage after the American fashion.

Paul Stanhope sat in his easy-chair, weary yet rejoicing. By his side, dressed in pure white, without ornament or gaudy color, but with a fresh loveliness superior to the charm of jewelry, Jennie stood tenderly holding his hand. Morgan stood on the other side of the invalid's chair, watching every motion he made, and as attentive to his friend as he could have been to his own mother.

The peculiar solemnity of the occasion touched every heart, and there was much quiet weeping by the sympathetic ladies, the compatriots of the bride and bridegroom. One of the visitors was an American clergyman making a tour around the world; a way of resting from the duties of a large pastorate suggested to him by his church, which also provided him the means to do it.

It was now his privilege to pronounce the words binding these faithful heroes together. The clergyman advanced until he stood before them, and repeated in low, clear tones the words of the marriage ceremony as it is spoken in America.

The couple in firm voices repeated the responses; the minister declared them united, and the prayer for the abiding blessing of God upon them was spoken. The people then crowded around the bridal couple with congratulations and good wishes. Both of them were smiling with serene appreciation of the kindness shown them. A soft, subtle happiness filled their souls. To both it seemed to be a foretaste of heaven. The simplicity of the ceremony impressed the Hindus present as being awfully sacred. They felt as if they were in the presence of the God of the missionaries.

From that moment Stanhope was thoroughly contented. He did not have another touch of homesickness. Yet he could hardly consent to have his bride out of his sight even for a moment. And she experienced a delight in serving him, in gratifying his every whim, in anticipating his wants, such as, when she reflected on it, gave her an idea of the nature of the love the Hindu women bore their husbands. At this moment she could have joyfully performed suttee to prevent her being separated from him. He absorbed her every thought. She wheeled his chair about on the veranda wherever he wanted it—sometimes where they could gaze on the white, glistening, snowy ranges; then in front of the lake, watching the happy pleasure parties as they enjoyed the boating;

or going to the other end of the veranda to watch the mountains below them or the mists rising up from the jungles and the plains. She read to him, and when he became weary rested his head on her bosom while he slept. Then she told him stories as she would have done to a little child, and he enjoyed them; their simplicity rested him. Thus it continued until one morning, as he sat in his chair looking over the great plain so far below them, talking of his work and of India becoming a garden for the Lord, his words sank to a whisper, and he ceased to speak. His wife knew his hour had come. Morgan was standing by her side, full of sympathy and devoted to their interests. Gently the two sustained the form of the missionary as, with a slight gasp, the life passed away and the weary worker entered into rest. In that hour of trial Jennie learned how thoughtful, tender, and helpful Morgan could be. A sister could not have smoothed her pathway more gently, and, trusting him thoroughly, she passed through the waters of affliction in the solemn communings of her own soul.

Every one about her manifested the greatest tenderness. Loving-kindness greeted her at every step; caresses, fond words, thoughtful acts, were all showered upon her. Every American and English heart was zealous to brighten her way and dispel her sorrow. The Hindus had never before seen the manner in which the Americans treated widows, and, curious to know, watched every motion that was made.

They buried the dead beneath a tree at the foot of the mountain, in a little cemetery there, and marked his grave with a small marble tablet. The Hindus noticed that the widow did not alter her attire nor lessen the number of her garments. The rings her husband gave her she still wore. Her hair was not cut off, but dressed as she had been accustomed to dress it. She was not put to hard menial labor, nor slighted by the happier ones, nor addressed with harsh words and phrases, but the most considerate tenderness was lavished upon her, and every lady called her darling, while the gentlemen could not be more thoroughly polite.

For a few days she continued near the grave of her beloved; then the desire to be at her work came upon her, and she prepared to return and take it up just where she had laid it down. The smiles came back to her pretty face, and the beauty of her faith was reflected in all her actions. When she spoke of her beloved, it was of one living with God in eternal blessedness, whither she was also going.

One morning Morgan bade her farewell for a short trip among the mountains. When he should return they would proceed to Agra. She saw him disappear up the valley, with his rifle over his shoulder, and his guide walking on before. She waited for his return, but at the time appointed he did not come. Days passed, and yet he came not. At length, with fear that some accident had befallen him in the mountain-recesses, she sent out searchers, but they returned without a trace of his movements. Burdened with this sorrow, one of doubt and foreboding, she sadly returned to Agra.

CHAPTER XXII.

PERILS IN THE MOUNTAINS.

MORGAN left the sanitarium to enjoy a ramble for a few days in one of the grandest regions on the earth—a region where nature reveled in greatness, toward which the millions of India's teeming population looked for evidences of the greatness of their gods. Lofty mountain-peaks seemed to be brought close together, and snowy ranges appeared at hand, yet their summits were so far away that days of traveling would be required to reach them. On every hand were crags and precipices, and deep chasms and ravines cutting into the immense ridges. In some places the fossil remains of gigantic creatures of a former age were found in vast beds; in others, nature displayed her richness of verdure and vegetation unsurpassed elsewhere in her broad dominions.

The vast forests and jungles were full of wonders. Tigers, leopards, and wild elephants, singly and in families, roamed through the forests, enjoying the freedom of the wild life into which they had been born.

Morgan was well supplied with ammunition, and, following his guide, went cheerfully deeper into the dense thickets covering the mountain sides. He did not apprehend danger from man, and trusted in his skill and the precision of his rifle to defend himself from the attack of wild beasts. He was entering a region where thousands of pilgrims came to worship the sources of the sacred rivers Ganges and Jumna, for, in the deep gorges of these mountains, the head-waters of the streams were honored as the most sacred spots on the earth. The jungle paths were littered with the traces of pilgrims.

Many, while searching for the sacred places, lost their way, and died through want and exposure; many defenseless travelers became the victims of tigers, or wolves, or poisonous serpents. Some succeeded in accomplishing their pilgrimage, and returned to the plains below to tell of the horrors surrounding the journey to the sources of their sacred streams.

Morgan penetrated the forests deeper and deeper, enjoying the scenery and an occasional battle with wild beasts, until the time set for his outward trip was exhausted, then he signaled his guide to lead the way back again. When no answers were given his signals, and the hours of waiting wore away, the thought that he was forsaken came to the hunter's mind. His guide had disappeared. In an unknown, uninhabited wilderness, he was alone. The sense of solitude was awful. As he reflected, he remembered that the guide was a stranger who had come to Nynee Tal about the same time as himself, and that he was entirely unknown to the people of that place. He had forced himself into Morgan's presence, and appearing to take a fancy to him, was always on hand to serve him. Morgan now recalled the conversations in which this man had suggested to him the pleasures of such a trip, advising him to take it, presenting as inducements the prospect of seeing herds of wild elephants and of drinking from the head-waters of the sacred rivers of India, where, in thousands of cascades, the waters leaped from the Himalayan glaciers to form the Ganges and the Jumna.

As he looked about, Morgan realized that he must do something. He did not know just how to go, for, trusting to his guide, he had given his attention to other things than the pathway through the undergrowth. With earnest purpose he tried to retrace his steps, hoping to get to some spot from which he could see some of the mountain-peaks known to him, and by them direct his course. At length, weary with walking, he cast himself down by the edge of a cliff to rest, and while resting feast his eyes on the beauties of the immense expanse of country stretching out before him.

The evening was rapidly advancing, and the atmosphere was of such rarity that he could see a great distance over the plains of India. The Ganges, like a silver thread, with towns along its banks and the plains dotted with hundreds of villages, was spread out before him, and India seemed to be larger and broader than he had ever before thought of its being. His thoughts began to measure the territories over which he had traveled and the seas he had crossed, and new conceptions of the greatness of the earth rushed upon him. He thought of the millions of men toiling like ants to obtain food from the earth. Then he thought of individuals. "What is man, that thou art mindful of him?" his mind asked with new force. Then came questions of destiny. Why was a man so splendidly endowed for usefulness as Paul Stanhope cut off before any one could see the good he had done? Why was Jennie Thompson, the loveliest woman he had ever met—and he was accustomed to the society of lovely women—burdened with grief and disappointments when she needed all the strength and help which a strong, wise, faithful man could give her? "God's ways are past finding out," he said, as if speaking in explanation to another. To his surprise, a hollow laugh from the bushes back of him greeted his words. Startled, he leaped to his feet, and with rifle in readiness looked about him, but all was silent as before, and there was not a sign of a living creature near him.

Now, for the first time, he noticed carefully the spot upon which he was standing. It was only a broad place in the narrow path, which wound around the face of an immense crag. Below him was a precipice hundreds of feet in depth; behind him a wall of rock perpendicular in front and utterly inaccessible to human climber. On the right and the left the path narrowed to only a goat's track across the cliff.

Impelled by his ardent admiration of nature's sublimity, he had come to this spot, and had forgotten his danger and isolation in contemplating the magnificent scene spread before him.

Again he heard the mocking laughter, and a moment after beheld a man advance along the narrow path toward him. It was the fakir who had threatened him with death. For a few moments the strange being glared at him with a sort of fierce delight, then, extending his long bony finger toward him, said, "Stranger, you can go no farther on that path; it ends at the edge of the cliff just beyond the crag, where the wild goats leap down to another path on the face of the cliff and pursue their way. A man cannot make that leap; only the wild goats can do it, and they often fail, dashing themselves on the rocks far below. Stranger, return, and learn the fate in store for those who hate the gods, defile temples, and steal the daughters of India."

Morgan looked around him, and saw that the fakir had told the truth about the path. Placing his rifle on his arm ready for instant use, he followed the fakir into the forest, and there, to his astonishment, beheld a group of fakirs sitting in a circle and grinning at him with the most hideous ferocity.

The beauty of a tiger's fur and the grace of its

motin awaken admiration—all the wild animals of the forest have attractive features—but here was a company of men, vile, foul, and abnormal; human hyena, shaving lost all sense of cleanliness and tenderness. A shudder passed over Morgan's manly form as he realized that he was in their power and utterly unable to save himself. For a moment he thought of resistance; he could at least kill a few of them, but he gave up the thought, for he knew they were quick and hardy, and should he injure any one of them he would but insure his own speedy destruction. By temporizing he might find a way of escape; at least this was the only hope he could see. Assuming a careless, curious manner, he saluted them, and began to ask them questions about the country they were in. "How far is it to the sources of the Ganges?" "Do many make pilgrimages there?" "Are you a company of holy men seeking rest by the sacred stream?" and similar questions.

But they only grinned at him, as if it were a joke; and in their grinning he read the expression of their merciless nature. Morgan had read of the Thugs of India, a sect of religious fanatics who worshiped Kalee, the consort of Shiva. Calcutta was named for her—Kalee-Ghat, or Kalee's Ghat, the place of Kalee's ablutions.

These fanatics honored her by shedding blood. The Kalika Purana describes her appetite for blood and carnage as follows: "If a devotee should scorch some member of his body by applying a burning lamp, the act would be very acceptable to the goddess; if he should draw some of his blood and present it, it would be still more delectable; if he should cut off some portion of his own flesh and present it as a burnt-offering, that would be most grateful of all. But if the worshiper should present her a whole burnt-offering it would prove acceptable to her in proportion to the supposed importance of the animated beings thus immolated: that, for instance, by the blood of fishes or tortoises the goddess is gratified for a whole month after; a crocodile's blood will please her three months; that of certain wild animal nine months; a guana's, a year; an antelope's, twelve years; a rhinoceros's or tiger's blood, for a hundred years; but the blood of a lion or a *man* will delight her appetite for a thousand years! while by the blood of three men slain in sacrifice she is pleased a hundred thousand years."

The English goverment had suppressed Thuggism, but Morgan thought the lingering hopes of such a faith could not be suppressed by force of arms. Perhaps these fakirs were believers in Kalee, who watched in these dense forests to entrap travelers, and, without fear of detection, satiate the goddess with their blood.

The recollection of the Thugs did not tend to compose his nerves, but with a brave face and manner he returned their gaze, showing them, probably for the first time, a man alone and in their power, yet not afraid of them. After a while their leader, Morgan's enemy, addressed them by words and actions full of passion, in a language Morgan did not understand, and to him they all gave close attention. As the speaker worked himself into a state of frenzy, his hearers were similarly affected, and they cast the most ferocious glances upon the stranger, who stood so calmly awaiting the close of this strange scene.

Suddenly several of the fakirs leaped from their circle and sprang upon him, securely pinioning his arms behind his back. Then, surrounding him, they all together rushed into the forest.

As the darkness was falling they came to a cave with a small opening, into which they forced him to crawl, all following, until the cave was filled by them. Then a stone was put to the entrance to prevent wild beasts from entering during the night.

It was a terrible night. The small, half-closed entrance was the only place air could get in, and between Morgan and that opening lay the entire crowd of fakirs. When darkness had fairly settled upon the forest the wild beasts, smelling the presence of men, prowled about the opening, crying, growling, and fighting, putting their noses to the hole, and becoming more savage because of their being unable to get at the men. But the stench of the filthy fakirs and the foul atmosphere were worse than the noises of the animals. In the open air, with the atmosphere constantly in motion, the offensiveness of the dirty unwashed men could be endured if not too close at hand; but in the cave, to breathe their breath and be deprived of oxygen reminded Morgan of the horrible black-hole of Calcutta. He forgot the danger menacing his life through some overt act of his foes in the suffering from the foul atmosphere, and he was profoundly thankful when the light of day came in through the entrance and the fakirs crawled out. Without taking any food, they all continued their journeying until they came to what seemed to be a park in the forest.

The underbrush was cleared away, the trees were shaped by the skill of a gardener, and flowering bushes and fruit-trees grew in profusion. In the midst of a fine grove stood a castle, ancient in form, and built so solidly as to defy an ordinary siege. It was grim and threatening in appearance to the man now being hurried toward it. Back of it were a number of buildings for the housing of the servants and herds of the lord of the castle. There were houses for elephants, cages for tigers and leopards, kennels for dogs, and aviaries for birds. It was, in fact, the rendezvous for the possessions of a rajah reserved for extraordinary occasions. As Morgan passed along he saw in fenced inclosures elephants, camels, horses, and bullocks quietly feeding, and the thought occurred to him that he had seen these animals in the great parade at Agra.

As he was forced toward the castle he noticed the servants gazing upon him with great curiosity, and also numbers of fakirs who evidently were wards of the rajah. Some of these were Hindus, but the greater number were Mohammedans. Just as they hurried him into the castle he threw the stone given him by Nemorama's fakir friend into the lap of a Hindu fakir sitting by the door. It was now his only hope. Before he could observe how the fakir received it, the door closed and he was in the castle.

His fakir captors were left on the outside; but two servants clothed in livery beckoned him to follow them. They led him along the broad hall until they came to a stair-way, which they descended. At the foot of the steps his conductors lit a torch, and, leading him down another stair-way and along another hall, came to a door, which they opened. Having thrust him in, they closed and bolted it against him, and withdrew.

The darkness at first was appalling. After a few moments Morgan's courage revived, and he examined the cell in which he had been placed. From the number of steps he had descended he knew that it was considerably beneath the ground, and, from the hardness of the walls, that it was in a mass of rock. From the ceiling there came a slender ray of light. Looking toward it, he saw a long, narrow, slanting aperture extending to a place in the side of the castle wall some distance above the ground. This was the only avenue for light and fresh air to come into the cell. It was the golden ray of good cheer. Looking at the beam of light, Morgan said to himself: "It is not all darkness. God reigns, and this ray of light teaches me that he has not forgotten me."

Morgan was nearly famished for lack of food, but hour after hour passed before his solitude was broken. The ray of light had faded, and the darkness was dense even to blackness, when the door opened and a servant entered with food and drink for him. Morgan consumed the food greedily, and without a word the servant withdrew. Many hours again passed, and he slept the deep sleep of extreme fatigue.

When he awoke he was refreshed. The light was coming through the aperture, and even the sounds of shouting and revelry from the outer world were plainly heard. After a while the door of the cell was again opened, and the servant commanded Morgan to follow him into the presence of his master. Somehow the fear of death had passed from his mind, and he was impelled by eager curiosity to watch for each move in the exciting drama. With every sense alert, he followed his guide along the hall, up the stairway, through the corridor leading to the door of the castle, and then up several flights of steps to the top of the tower surmounting the castle. Here he was ushered into a room, the like of which he had never before seen. It was a summer-room, the roof being supported by strong pillars, and curtains extending from pillar to pillar to regulate the light and the currents of air.

The scenery from the curtained ways was the grandest Morgan had seen. On the one side were the Himalayan peaks of everlasting snow and great forests, while on the other side the view embraced hundreds of square miles of the fertile plains. It was a magnificent watch-tower, and an enemy could not approach it from any direction without being discovered in the far distance. In a hasty glance Morgan saw the course of the great highway of India, and his heart throbbed with hope as in the distance he beheld a train of cars moving on the North-western Railway of India in the plains below.

The room was fitted to suit the taste of a hunter. The floor was nearly covered with rugs made of tiger-skins, while the pillars were decorated with ornaments made of elephants' tusks, tigers' teeth and claws, and serpents' scales, all made brilliant with settings of precious stones. Upon an immense tiger-mat in the center of the room sat the rajah, the master of the castle, and Morgan at once recognized him as the chieftain whom he had seen at Agra.

The face of the rajah showed lust and brutality in every line, and Morgan shuddered as he thought of a maiden like Nemorama becoming the slave of such a being. All that art and wealth could do to make the rajah attractive had been done, and in the eyes of his servants he shone with unequaled magnificence. To them he was prince and lord. He wore a vest made of gold cloth, a coat of yellow satin, with a border of gold embroidery. A handsome cashmere shawl was loosely folded about his waist, and a puffy light turban was on his head. His trousers and stockings were of richest material, and from his turban to his shoes he was decorated with brilliant jewels. A fillet of diamonds and rubies ornamented his head, and a band of diamonds and rubies his girdle. All was beautiful except the man, and the costly gems of nature could not hide nor render attractive the base human soul which was revealed in his dull countenance.

When Morgan entered his presence he continued sitting on the mat, not deigning to notice his presence. After a short time he rang a little silver bell, and a servant hastened to him with a tray, upon which were glasses filled with refreshing drinks. Taking one of these, he slowly sipped it, and, turning his gaze toward the prisoner, coolly surveyed him from head to foot. As he did so there was profound silence in the room, the servants carefully watching every motion of their master, to anticipate his will before he should utter it in words.

As Morgan returned the rajah's gaze he was convinced that no appeal for mercy could reach that imbruted nature, and, with the grit of a thoroughly brave man, determined not to flinch, nor by word or act to crave a favor. Through an interpreter the rajah demanded "By what right have you, a stranger, stolen from her owners the beautiful maiden destined to shine as the light of the harem of the lord of the Himalayan forests?"

But Morgan kept silent.

The rajah motioned with his hand, and the fakir came forward, holding in his fingers the two bullets, which he had carefully preserved. Then he informed the rajah how he had obtained them, and the threat he had uttered to the prisoner as to the final use to be made of them. He told the story of Morgan's dealings with Nemorama, of his finding Kismut, and of his accomplices in his underhand work, ending with an account of the failure of the brigands working in the rajah's service to wrest Nemorama from the protection of the valorous Dennis.

Morgan was amazed at the accuracy of the fakir's information, but was delighted to hear of the success attending Dennis, for this encounter had happened since his last tidings from the faithful Irishman.

Finding that the prisoner would not answer a word, the rajah's face flushed with anger, and, holding the bullets before him, he said: "You will now be taken back to your cell, and to-morrow, at the hour of noon, will be led forth, and in front of the castle gate will be put to death in the manner the fakir has sworn. One ball will be shot into your head, because it planned so wicked a plot against the happiness of my harem, keeping it in darkness for the lack of the light of the beautiful one. The other ball will be shot into your heart, because it sought to steal the love and devotion that belongs only to me. Go!"

As he uttered this word the servants took hold of the prisoner and hurried him down the stair-ways. Shutting him in his cell, they left him to meditate in solitude and darkness the fate before him.

With a feeling of despair Morgan cast himself on the floor of the cell. He was alone—no one to appeal to, no friend to help. As he watched the slender ray of light coming through the aperture he saw it growing dimmer and dimmer, until it entirely faded out. Now that death seemed so near, his longing to live became the greater, and he thought of many plans to escape, but every one of them ended in hopelessness. His reveries were interrupted by the door of his cell being unbolted. As it opened he saw a man shrouded from head to foot in a fakir's shroud enter, carrying in his hand a little lamp. He shut the door after him, the servant accompanying him remaining on the outside.

The man then removed the shroud, and, to his amazement, Morgan beheld his friend, the Hindu fakir. The fakir, in low tones, bade him wrap himself in the shroud, in silence follow the servant out of the castle, turn to the right and walk into the forest, and do as he should there be instructed.

With deepest emotions of gratitude Morgan obeyed, and, knocking on the door, passed out as it was opened by the servant. The servant stopped only long enough to bolt the door of the cell securely, and then led the way to the castle door.

As Morgan stepped into the open air he gave thanks to God for his abundant mercies. The stars were shining brilliantly, and deep shadows were resting on the gardens and forests. The servants seemed to be all asleep, and without hinderance he entored the forest before him.

Almost at the edge of the wood he met a fakir, who directed him to follow. For many minutes they swiftly walked along the beaten path, and when the fakir stopped they stood by a broad road. The fakir then led a saddled horse out from the shelter of the trees, bade him mount the horse and ride with speed toward the south, and if he did not tarry he could reach the railroad in time to take the midnight train to the south. Morgan did as he was commanded. The horse was fleet of foot and strong in limb, and he galloped at a furious gait. For a full hour Morgan sped on, reached the railroad, and turned the horse loose just as the train came rolling rapidly along. In a few moments he was seated in the cars on his way to Bombay, and as he looked toward the lofty castle he wondered what would be the next scene in the drama of which he was so unwillingly an actor.

The Hindu fakir sat on the floor of the cell in silence. He did not care much if death did meet him, but he knew the rajah would not dare to put a fakir to death, however great the provocation. His superstition would prevent him, as well as the fear of the consequences that might follow. As he sat in silence he heard the approach of footsteps; in a moment the cell door opened, and the door closed as another fakir entered. The visitor was startled to see the Hindu. It was the Mohammedan fakir, who had come to taunt Morgan. For a moment the two fakirs glared at each other, the little flickering lamp casting its feeble light upon them. The Hindu uttered the words, "At last!" and the next moment they sprang at each other.

The ferocity of the fakirs was equal to that of wild beasts. They were utterly merciless, and, unless separated, a contest meant death to one or to both. Now they were alone. In the closeness of the cell the sound of their battling was repressed. The servants of the castle were sleeping, dreaming, perhaps, of the interesting execution on the morrow. Not long afterward the Hindu opened the door, and, with the lamp in his hand, passed out of the castle.

The following morning, when all was arranged for the execution, the rajah sent to the cell for his prisoner. The servants with torches hastened, and, entering the cell, saw the Mohammedan, dead. Filled with fear, they returned to their master, and when the body was brought forth a superstitious awe swept over them all. No one could give a word of explanation.

It was one of the mysteries of the dealings of the gods. The rajah, frightened by it, immediately ordered the howdah to be placed on his elephant for him to go to Agra to consult the wise hakims as to the significance of this event.

16

CHAPTER XXIII.

IN THE HEART OF INDIA.

DENNIS was very anxious to report himself to Captain Grey. It is true he had sent many letters describing the events he passed through, but he had not heard from the captain, and as his route must be taken according to circumstances, he could not tell where he would be a week in advance.

He began to feel badly, too, from the injuries he had received in the battle on the highway. At the time his courage and the necessity of protecting the ladies in his charge had enabled him to disguise his real condition. But, riding along quietly in the palanquin, he had an opportunity of considering his own feelings, and he concluded that he was going to be sick. They were now traveling through Malway, a country in which the land gradually rose toward the Vindhya Mountains. It was a country almost devastated by the brigand hordes of petty chieftains previous to the English supremacy, but since then the enforced peace and security obtained for all had wonderfully developed its resources. As they passed through it Nemorama interested her companions by reciting to them the exploits of Vicramaditya, one of the early Hindu kings, of whom the most stirring, fabulous accounts were given. It was a part of India in which the Mohammedans failed to make much headway, and when the Mahrattas entered it in the defense of the real Hindu faith they were received with open arms.

At length the travelers reached Oojein, a city on the north side of the mountains, and on a branch of the Chumbul River. It is historically a place of great importance, holding high rank as one of the sacred cities of the Puranas, and Hindu geographers had fixed upon it as their first meridian. In ancient times it was a great interior capitol, until a change in the course of the river nearly ruined it. The Mohammedans have built several very handsome mosques, and the great caravans passing through make it one of their principal stations. It was in this territory that Allah Baiee for twenty years proved to be the greatest ruler the country had ever had, and showed to all India that a woman knew how to rule.

As they reached this city, Nemorama saw that it was impossible for the sick man to travel further, and finding a house in a pleasant garden for rent, she had Dennis conveyed thither, and with the assistance of Kismut tried to nurse him back to health again.

Multitudes of people were constantly passing the little whitewashed mud cottage in which the travelers had found refuge—Mohammedans on the way to their decorated mosques, Hindus going to their jewel-crowned pagodas, merchants with the products of all India brought to them by great caravans, elephants used for labor, camels from long journeys, white bullocks drawing little carriages, and crowds of people. It was thoroughly a Hindu city, and the whole tone of life was according to the rules laid down by the white-robed Brahmans.

The fear of pursuit had departed. The travelers knew that the natural jealousies between the various rajahs would be a defense to them from the schemes of the northern powers, and they were no longer afraid. Nevertheless, they continued in disguise. Having given up the Hindu religion for that of Christ, they cast aside the marks of caste and clan, and recognized all people as their equals. Nemorama was no longer a nautchnee, but a Hindu maiden; Kismut was no longer a widow, but a Hindu woman; and in the ordinary dress of the better class of Hindus, they modestly went forward doing the duties before them. Dennis now observed, as never before, the distinguishing trait of the Hindu woman's character. They were said to excel as nurses, and, in fact, in any position where devotion and gentleness were required.

Nemorama assumed the general charge of affairs. She visited the markets and attended to all the outside duties, while Kismut did the nursing and the cooking. Their tread was so light as they passed through the room that they seemed almost as visions floating before the sick man, and lying on his cot, he watched them and wove fancies about them, in which the most delightful surprises were constantly appearing.

Nemorama knew a little of bruises, for in the nautchnee home accidents were frequent, and with her skillful touch she dressed the sufferer's wounded head and prevented inflammation from setting in. Kismut was constantly near him. She stood motionless as a statue when no service was required, then, when needed, she moved noiselessly and quickly. She did not allow an insect to rest upon him for an instant, and insects were thickly swarming all about them. Not a fly nor a mosquito could reach him. When he slept Kismut used her fan so constantly that a gentle breeze seemed to be fanning his cheeks, and although the heat was intense throughout the city and he was painfully susceptible to it, yet she drove away its exhausting attacks and gave him a constant current of air. As a cook she had been well trained, and her dishes of curry could not be surpassed. The arrangement of the food was so neat and pretty that it encouraged his appetite, and he ate freely, while she stood smiling upon him and keeping away the flies.

Dennis realized, as he became stronger, that only careful nursing had brought him through, and with all his heart he loved the gentle woman who had saved his life.

O how sweet and attractive she appeared to him, as

hour after hour he fondly gazed upon her! He knew something of married life in his own country, and he had seen brawling, noisy, contentious couples, where the household was in perpetual strife and discord. So he had preferred living a life of single blessedness and remaining the confidential servant of Captain Grey. But now a vision of another kind of life floated before his mind. He saw a woman full of the spirit of love consecrating all her powers of heart, mind, and body to the preservation of peace and rest within her house, and finding her greatest delight in the happiness of her household. As he watched Kismut he saw that to her it was not work nor bondage, but her pleasure, her ardent delight, and he could not possibly help yielding her his admiration and affection.

When Captain Grey again heard from his faithful servitor Dennis was rapidly recovering, and as soon as he was able the party resumed their journey toward Bombay. The captain, anxious to help Dennis, came with all the speed camels could make to meet him in Oojein, and arrived the day after the travelers had left. However, he soon overtook them, to the intense delight of Dennis and the satisfaction of his companions.

The women were modestly veiled, and the captain could see only the lower portion of their faces; but he greeted them with a friendliness that showed his sympathy with the mission Dennis was executing. As they traveled together Dennis opened his heart to the captain. He said: "An' it was just this way. I niver thought of a haythen woman other than one in perpetual darkness, that didn't know any thing but to spend all her time before idols and all her thoughts in the worship of thim dirty fakirs. Whin I see'd their mud cottages I thought they couldn't be possessed wid refinement or sinse, and I was greatly prejudiced against thim. Whin Mr. Morgan axed me to help him out of a scrape, sure an' I was ready to sarve a man so brave as he was, an' I had no suspicion that within my own bosom my heart was sensitive. But, captain, truly now, ye may laugh at me if ye will, but I niver in all me born days saw so much swateness in a human crayture as that Kismut possesses. Such arnestness, such devotion, an' all the time so smilin' like; an' no matter how pervarse I would be, she niver by word or token gave ividence of bein' disturbed; an' it is just such a swate, illigant crayture that my heart goes out after; an' I am sure that with her a-lovin' me as long as I live, I shall be the happiest of men."

The captain did not laugh at his man, but rode on in silence for some time. Dennis watched him, and saw an expression of unutterable sadness cross his face, and even tears rolling down his cheeks. Not knowing what to think of it, he remained silent.

After a while the captain came to his side again and said: "Dennis, my boy, I think Kismut must be very beautiful, and all that you say of her I believe to be true; take her and be happy with her. I was just thinking of my own Hindu wife, and my heart was filled with lonesomeness because I must live without her.

"Dennis, I have seen a great many women. I have known them in nearly all parts of the world. I have seen them at home and abroad; I have watched all kinds of social customs, and I must say that I know of no women anywhere who are the equals, as a class, to the high-caste Hindu women in the purely household virtues. They are not educated; they are very devout; they are great sufferers when affliction comes upon them; they are slighted and too often despised by men; they are really a down-trodden sex. Yet, for all that, in purity of life, in affection for their husbands, in zeal for the virtues of their homes, in care for their children, they are superior to nearly all other women.

"Now, a man marries generally for love in our country, hence no wife can be more gratifying than a noble Hindu woman. A Hindu marries to become the father of sons; if he does not become such, his happiness is wrecked, and his life for time and for eternity is a failure. What a pity it is that the Hindus do not marry for love, when their women are so loving and faithful!"

"An' how do yez account for their loving sperit?" asked Dennis.

Captain Grey replied: "I partly account for it on the theory of their training. They have been taught that their only hope of heavenly enjoyment is in devotion to their husbands. They have also been taught that it is a great disgrace for a girl to be without a husband. And the rule is to spend their time from nine years of age until they are fourteen or sixteen in learning from the mother-in-law how to serve their husbands, and they are generally married to men twice or three times their own age. And youth is taught to reverence age. All these features of their training have developed them in the domestic line, and their affection for their husbands partakes of the nature of worship."

"I understand," said Dennis. "An' I think the Hindus are not sech haythen, after all, but rather scriptural, for they follow the words of Paul whin he spakes to thim, 'Husbands, love your wives; wives, obey your husbands.' An' I think to follow that rule would bring peace to many hurt souls."

"Yes," replied the captain; "and if they were to follow that precept in our home land it would gradually lead women to refuse to marry men whom they could not respect and obey and trust.

Thus the men conversed as they rode along following the palanquins in which the ladies were riding. At length they arrived in Bombay, and while the captain returned to his mountain home, Dennis sought a house where the ladies could dwell until they should receive news of Morgan. The varied busy life of the great city, with its different nationalities, was a constant wonder to the gentle Kismut. To Nemorama it was home; but while home she kept her face hidden whenever she went out of the house, for if discovered by her former friends she might be remanded into a captivity which would now be worse than death.

They were there only a few days when Dennis came to them with his face sparkling with excessive happiness. Making a profound bow to them, he said: "Ladies, it gives me great pleasure to inform yez that I have just had the honor of beholding the countenance of my esteemed friend Mister Morgan, an' he told me to inform yez that he would be here in half an hour."

With utterances of delight they pushed Dennis out of the way and rushed to their rooms to prepare to receive in a proper manner their beloved benefactor.

CHAPTER XXIV.

DASEE.

When Morgan reached Bombay, he hastened to Watson's Hotel to receive his letters from home and recruit his wearied body by rest, with all the conveniences of European skill about him. Then he sought his former friends to apprise them of his return and to form his plans for the coming season.

There was one place where he was particularly desirous of paying his respects, for in no other dwelling of the Hindus had he received so great kindness and polite attention. The house was on Malabar Hill, only a short distance below the Parsee Tower of Silence. Its grounds bordered on the broad public driveway —the principal resort of the wealthy people of Bombay when riding in their carriages. It was a place constantly fanned by the gentle breezes from the sea, and its richness of vines, trees, and shrubbery, with hundreds of musical birds singing about flowing fountains, made it a spot in which the highest charms of life could be enjoyed.

The refinement marking the outside of the house was excelled by the beauty, grace, and splendor of the life inside. Baboo Chunder, the Hindu owner of this beautiful place, was of a progressive spirit; and as he beheld the elegance and comforts enjoyed by the Europeans, endeavored to obtain equal advantages for himself, and by his example to induce his people to enjoy them. Being scrupulously exact in fulfilling all the observances of the Hindu laws, he was thus above reproach. With a strength of will and clearness of intellect rarely surpassed, he devoted his wealth and influence to the amelioration of his fellows and the elevation of the people of India. It was in his house that Morgan had for the first time witnessed the acting of the beautiful nautchnee; and now, having returned to Bombay, he sought the elegant mansion, to pay his respects to the people who had treated him so kindly.

Morgan's mind was recalling with great pleasure the lovely daughter of Baboo Chunder. Dasee was one of the rarest maidens of India, the pride of her father's house, the light of the zenana, and the envy of all the maidens of Malabar Hill. The zenana in Chunder's house was not at all like the zenanas of the ordinary Hindu homes. It was above spacious gardens, with a wealth of scenery from its broad, handsomely carved windows and balconies unsurpassed in Bombay. The view stretched over the city, over the bay, and to the distant inland shores, with their fringes of green, and the high hills beyond covered with blooming verdure.

In this zenana there was no exclusion of light, fresh air, and freedom, but the broadest privileges. The rooms were furnished with handsome rugs, works of art, and with the best literature of all ages and nations. Here Dasee reigned as a queen. Her beauty of person and grace of motion were in harmony with her surroundings. She seemed to be fitted perfectly to the elegance, wealth, and culture with which her father had surrounded her. The piano in her boudoir often gave evidence of her skill in music, and the comments found here and there on the margins of English, American, French, German, and Hindu books in the library showed the wide extent of her reading and the analytical skill with which she weighed the thoughts of the learned writers. Morgan had been attracted by her brightness, and through her courtesy he learned that some zenanas in India were the equals of the most palatial homes in America.

When Morgan reached the mansion he sent in his card, and was received in the spacious parlor looking out upon the ocean. A Hindu woman came to meet him, whom he recognized as Dasee's attendant, and he quickly saw that her face was disturbed by some great sorrow. The tears had been freely flowing, and had left their traces upon the cheeks of the expressive face. As Morgan listened, the woman told of the grief that had come to their house. Baboo Chunder was dead. He had died suddenly. In usual health in the morning, he had kissed his daughter and had gone to his business. Before noon his lifeless body was returned to his home. There was a great funeral, and the body was consumed upon a funeral pyre, built of the most precious aromatic woods. His daughter had laid many valuable jewels upon the altar in his favorite temple, and mourned his loss with all the grief of her first sorrow or stroke of misfortune.

This was only the beginning of their troubles, and the light of the house was in gloom and in danger of being quenched. Baboo Chunder was a high-caste Hindu, zealous for the customs of his people. When Dasee was nine years of age, according to the custom, he married her to a youth just twice her age, the son of a Hindu equal in caste and clan, and having such advantages as would give promise of a suitable and prosperous union. The horoscopes were declared propitious, the Brahman priests encouraged it, and it received the approval of the people generally.

One condition, however, was exacted, which was that Dasee should remain in her father's house, and that the youth should also dwell there and be educated by Baboo Chunder, until Dasee reached her development and was of a suitable age to be given to him. These conditions were agreed to, and the marriage took place. Dasee had never seen the youth before. She knew nothing of the serious nature of the marriage. She had no choice in it, but, like any girl of her age, enjoyed the display, the revelry, and the feastings attending it.

But the conditions were at once violated. The

parents of the young man removed from Bombay to Benares, and took their son with them. They demanded possession of Dasee, but this her father positively denied them, and in his own house gave her the most thorough education that the learned pundits could impart to her. Day by day she grew in grace, beauty, and in the powers of intellect. Sanskrit was her delight. She inherited her father's rare intellectual powers and poetic love of all that was beautiful, and under the guidance of the pundits became the favorite of the most learned circle in Bombay.

On the other hand, the youth to whom she was married, filled with arrogance because of his spotless pedigree, vainly glorying in the sacred thread proclaiming his caste, followed in the way of his fathers in sacrificing every thing to preserve inviolate that caste distinction. He had no taste for literary studies, and, ignorant of the advantages of culture, grew up a narrow-minded, bigoted, heartless man. He was proud of his caste, his poverty, his few wants. Boorish in manners and vacant in thought, he gazed with supreme admiration upon the filthy fakirs as his models of the true kind of a life, and accepted with equal pleasure the adulation of the people of lower castes. His idea of wives and of women in general was the common one among his fellows. They were only to serve their husbands, to eat what he left on his plate, to stand behind him and brush the flies away so that they should not touch his sacred body, to submit to whatever request he might make, or give instant obedience to his commands. All their blessedness was to be in serving him, and if they violated his least command they were eternally shut out from heaven. His smile could unlock heaven, and his frown close it forever against them. Such were his thoughts, and his pride rose higher and higher as he contemplated the time when he could command the obedience of the lovely Dasee.

Many times he sent demands that she be given to him, but Baboo Chunder, watching how he had been trained, refused, and contemplated with horror putting his daughter, accustomed only to love, gentleness, and refinement, into the hands of such a cruel fanatic. The subject was never mentioned to his daughter, and only a dim recollection of it remained in her mind. She had seen her husband but once—that was the time of the marriage—and since then all her thoughts had turned in other directions. It was impossible for the youth or his parents to obtain her while Chunder stood in the way; but he died. Immediately after her father's funeral the husband appeared and claimed his wife.

Dasee was appalled. She did not know the man, neither did she wish to know him after giving one glance at his brutal face, marked by ignorance and selfishness. She had no love for him, and it would be impossible for her to ever learn to love him. To be the slave of such a man was worse than death. It shocked every conception she entertained of purity and refinement. She felt that she could not leave her beautiful home and live in a mud cottage, to spread cow ordure on the walls once a week and in the yard about the cottage every day. Thus to consecrate her life to the one thing of serving such an ignoramus! But he was inflexible. He did not care for gold nor jewels; he despised them. Nothing would satisfy him but possession of the maiden. The laws of Manu said, "Whatever be the qualities of the man with whom a woman is united in lawful marriage, such qualities even she assumes, like a river united with the ocean."

The recollection of this law filled her soul with dread. As she looked at him she asked herself, in horror, if she could ever sink so low as to be known by the possession of such infamous and despicable qualities. She pleaded for release or for compromise, but he was deaf to all pleadings. With lordly pride he commanded her to obey him. Then she refused, positively and finally. His friends advised him to carry the matter to the courts. He did so, and the courts were compelled to decide according to the law. The law was in his favor, and the common prison was the only alternative to obedience. The judges said Dasee must go either with her husband or to the prison. With calm resignation, such as touched all hearts, Dasee replied to the judges, "Send me to prison if you will; I shall never go with that man as his wife."

The decision had been rendered, the judgment pronounced, and Dasee was at once led to prison. O what a change from the sweet, pure air on Malabar Hill, where loving thought and wealth had surrounded her with every luxury, to the narrow, bare cell, with the worst of convicts and criminals, the lowest and vilest wretches, with their curses and vile shouts ringing in the air! But terrible as this was, she felt safe from defilement. Within her cell she could be true to her ideal of pure womanhood. Brave in heart, she resisted all the efforts of the cruel monster to possess her, and in devotions daily fortified her honorable soul.

The hot days of summer came—the season in which she had always gone to the mountains to escape the oppressive heat. Morgan was with the missionaries at Nynee Tal, but Dasee was still in the prison. How long could she endure it?

As Morgan listened to this story of his lovely friend he was inexpressibly shocked, and he went from the house asking himself, "Is there not some way to save Dasee from this awful calamity?"

CHAPTER XXV.

VICTORY IN DEATH.

MORGAN was hastening toward the hotel, when he saw before him the smiling face of the trusty Irishman.

"Hello, Dennis! Is that you?" he said; and Dennis, looking at him a moment, grasped the outstretched hand as he replied: "Be me sowl, an' this is Mister Morgan; but I would not 'a' known yez for the distrestful look upon your face. But cheer up, for the ladies are here in Bombay, an' safe at that; an', what is more, Mister Morgan, they are achen all over to see yez. Sure an' 'tis myself that is the happy man to lead yez to thim."

Morgan was delighted with the success that attended Dennis's efforts, and, after going to his hotel, followed him to the cottage where the maidens were temporarily living.

His meeting the women whom he had so greatly befriended was the most awkward moment of his life. How to salute them he did not know, neither did they, and if it had not been for Dennis no one can tell what mistakes might have been made; but the jolly Irishman began to express pleasure enough for the entire party. His wit set them all a-laughing, and the laughter hid the embarrassment they all felt. Then it became necessary for each one to know the experiences of the other, and the day wore away. Morgan could not think of leaving until a dish of curry was disposed of, and then Nemorama somehow held him until the stars were brightly shining above them. When he did return to his hotel he knew not which was greater, his happiness in seeing Nemorama or his sorrow over the calamities that had befallen Dasee.

The next morning he hastened to the cottage to instruct Dennis to leave Bombay immediately with the ladies, and go to the mountain home of Captain Grey, for the cholera had broken out in the city, and before many days every cottage on the mountains would be occupied by the people fleeing from the awful scourge. After seeing them depart for the mountains, Morgan began his efforts for the release of Dasee.

The European residents of Bombay were unanimous in condemnation of the law, and their ardent sympathies were aroused in behalf of the maiden, whom many of them knew and loved so well. They pleaded with the judges to mitigate the sentence, but they found themselves opposed by the iron hand of custom and the firm hand of the law.

The Hindus of Bombay sided with the husband. They claimed that he had the right to his wife, and the most terrible consequences would befall her if she did not submit to his commands. She should honor him because of the purity of his caste, and her rebellion was because her father had trained her in the luxuries of the English, and apart from the customs of her people. The Hindus, therefore, besought the judges to let the law take its course, and the refractory maiden be fully punished. Thus Morgan found that he could do nothing, and that the very features of the maiden's life that aroused his compassion had the opposite effect upon the Hindus. Her conduct was subversive of all their customs.

Meanwhile the cholera spread rapidly. In the densely populated districts of the city its ravages were terrible, and a sort of gloom seemed to settle upon the people. Crime increased in the infected districts, and the officers of the law had their hands full in trying to preserve peace and order among the people in the slums. Deprived of exercise and proper food and air, Dacee was growing physically weaker and weaker. Evidently the seeds of disease were fastening upon her system, but her clear, noble countenance was growing serener and more spiritual day by day. She cast off her Hindu faith when she entered the prison. The words of Jesus stored in her mind now proved to be a treasury of delight. The contemplation of the rewards God bestowed upon the faithful filled her soul with rapture. As the ravages of the cholera increased, and crime with it, the prison became overcrowded. The filth and vileness brought within the gates was horrible, and Dasee often felt faint as, from the language used by these wretches, she learned how low human beings could descend. These wretches from the cholera-stricken slums not only brought their cursings, but also the cholera, and it began to rage within the prison. O, what a place the prison then became! The curses of the imprisoned wretches, the shrieks of the manacled, the cries of those who were attacked by the dreaded disease, and the heavy measured tramp of the guards bringing in the criminals and carrying out the dead kept up the constant excitement. The air of the prison was laden with the stench of the wretches, which no amount of cleansing could remove. Forced to breathe such an atmosphere, the maiden, unusually susceptible to disease germs because of her feeble condition, became a victim, and, after a few hours of intense suffering, died. When she died she was alone. To the prison officials she was no more than any other prisoner. They did not know nor care about her crime. Without tender hands to serve her in her need, or gentle words of love whispered in her ear, or sympathetic friends to weep at her sufferings, drawn up with pain and in awful agony, she gasped out her last breathings, and only when the warden came with the scanty portion of food daily given her was her death known.

Tramp, tramp, tramp, came the guards and stood by the prison doors, while other prisoners rudely dragged the bodies of the dead out of the gate, and threw them in a heap on the dead-cart. The body of the beautiful Dasee was served the same as the vilest wretches, and the cart, full of corpses, was sent to the burning ghaut, where the bodies of brutal criminal and the gentle maiden were together consumed, and the ashes left to be the sport of the wind and the weather. When the news of her death was made known, Morgan again left Bombay, and followed his wards up the mountain-sides.

Captain Grey's head-quarters were in an old Mahratta fortress situated on the top of one of the lofty round-top hills of the Western Ghauts.

It was a place famous for being the field of some of Sejani's brilliant exploits, and the whole surrounding country was awake to traditions of the skill and valor displayed by that wonderful chieftain in defending the mountain districts against the Mohammedan invaders under the celebrated Mogul Aurungzebe. Romance took the place of history, and the wildest tales of adventure and of love were related in the zenanas, with Sejani as the captivating and ever-successful hero. The place given to Captain Grey was on the upper side of a precipitous hill, rendering the fort almost impregnable. So thought Sejani's foes when they possessed it. But he climbed the dizzy height, fastened a rope-ladder to the top ledge, and, going down the rope, commanded his followers to climb the rope and capture the fortress. The first man refused the hazardous undertaking, and Sejani immediately plunged his dagger into the man's heart. Without a word the rest of his men obeyed, and the surprised garrison awoke only to die; and thus his enemies learned that no place was impregnable when Sejani attacked it. Now in English hands, the old fortress was changed into comfortable barracks; the science of defense was applied to strengthen the place, so that if war should again break out in India not even the skill of a Sejani would be able to wrest the fortress from its English defenders. Under the shadow of the fort was established a hospital, and the grounds about the buildings were made as attractive as the skill of English gardeners using the flora of that part of India could make them.

The frequent spectacle of invalid soldiers resting beneath the shady trees or walking along paths bordered by fragrant, blooming bushes gave evidence of the value of this mountain sanitarium to the brave men who held India in subjection to the highest type of European civilization. The hospital was located here because of the purity of the atmosphere and the refreshing coolness while the cities in the lowlands were sweltering in heat. It was far above the line of fevers and cholera and the various diseases peculiar in India. Here men became strong again, and realized the pleasure of living where nature contributed to her fullest measure in supplying the blessings of life. The place had been accidentally discovered by an English officer when on a hunting expedition.

As the beauties of the place burst unexpectedly upon his view, he stopped to examine the various features it presented, and became enraptured with the excellences of its atmosphere and surroundings. Below, all along the road leading to it—a road passing yawning chasms and bridging rushing streams—were numbers of Hindu temples, many of them in ruins.

In the older days, before the English came, this road was a highway for pilgrims, such as pious Hindus, learned Brahmans, and sacred fakirs, who located themselves by these chasms or behind the jutting crags, and received the adoration of the common people, who toiled up the steep mountain to their sacred cloisters. Here, also, in the more secluded spots, apart from the din and frivolity of the world, men consecrated themselves to the study of the sacred Vedas, and sought to sever their affections from the world, that they might be endowed with keenes spiritual illumination. But the hermits retired into deeper solitudes when the sacredness of their resorts was broken into by the unscrupulous curiosity of adventurous foreigners. They left their temples to fall into decay, while in the depths of the mountains or at the head fountains of sacred streams the holy men in poverty re-established themselves, and, with a power they never lost, still attracted the ambitious youths of Hindu households.

It was along this road that Dennis led the women, not now carried in palanquins, but walking, for they left the city in haste.

Dennis knew the road well, and many a merry tale he told them of the battles along the road between the servants of the various temples in their efforts to win the pilgrims passing by. When they arrived near the hospital—a place generally shunned by the Hindus—they found a cottage which would answer their purposes very well, and here, for a small rental, they established themselves, Dennis going up to the fortress to serve the captain, as he had been accustomed to doing.

It was in this cottage that Morgan found them as he came up the road, followed by hundreds of Europeans fleeing from Bombay until the cholera season should pass away. As he looked into their bright, happy faces, he felt repaid for all that he had done for them, and with the promise to visit them on the morrow, continued his journey up the hill to the grim old fortress which guaranteed security to them all.

CHAPTER XXVI.

A HINDU'S LOVE.

EDWARD MORGAN was cordially greeted by Captain Grey, and at once installed in one of the best rooms in the fortress. There, as every-where, army officers in their permanent quarters lived in luxury. With plenty of male servants to do their bidding, the government to pay the bills, discipline exacting from every one a rigid observance of the military code, and not too much to do, they had every opportunity for enjoying a life suitable to their occupation.

Morgan was charmed with the scenery from the ramparts of the fortress. Back of them for a great distance tops of scores of hills were seen, peaks of every form and size, separated by deep ravines, interspersed here and there by graceful water-falls, where the mountain streams forced their way from one ravine down to another. In front of them they beheld hill-side and plain; great groves of lofty palms; forests of delicate cypress; orchards of peaches and other luscious fruits, gardens of coffee, tea, cinchona, and other cultivated shrubs; little villages here and there; temples rose every-where. Beyond all, under a haze or vapor which seemed to be floating in the air, giving it a blue color, rolled the distant and limitless sea. Morgan, looking along the winding road, could plainly see the cottage occupied by his friends, and he felt that from this place the course they were to pursue in the future must be marked out.

As they were talking about the strange life of the people of India, with its many mysteries and contradictions, the captain related to his guests the story * of one whom he had seen but a few days before:

"On one of the hills we can see from the summit of our fortress stands the temple of Khandoba, the warrior-god of the ancient Mahrattas. This temple is served by many girls or young women. One of the beautiful priestesses of the temple fell in love with a young Mahratta noble. She was heart-broken when his visits suddenly ceased, and she sent a message by a sudra, a male attendant serving the temple, to her lover, assuring him of her deep love for him, and her desire to escape from the temple and serve him even as a slave in his household.

"The sudra was also in love with the girl, and instead of delivering her message, he told her falsely that her lover had advised her to be happy where the gods had placed her. He hoped to gain her for himself. The following morning the girl was missed, and on the next day her body, all crushed and mangled, was found at the foot of a precipice called

* This story is given in the book *Life and Travels in India*, by Anna H. Leonowens. It is given here to illustrate a phase of Hindu character needed to complete one's understanding of that wonderful people.

Dewanee-garh, her lota or drinking-vessel still tied to her neck. Months after the Mahratta noble came again to the temple, and learned the sad fate of the girl. He had not deserted her, but had gone on a sacred pilgrimage to Benares, and had just returned. He was so affected by the story of her death that he took the battered lota in his hands and swore to perform the 'Gala Naik,' the severest course of asceticism known among the Hindus. He went to the edge of the precipice from which the girl had flung herself, and there he stood, with his head thrown back, gazing at the sun and holding the lota in his hand.

"The priestesses pitied him and took him food, and there he stood until reason gave way. Since then he remains part of the time perched on the verge of the precipice, other times wandering on the hill-side, but always holding in his hand the battered lota.

"When I saw him the other day his long hair, partly gray, hung in masses on his shoulders; his hands and feet, with nails like talons, looked like huge claws; his body was emaciated, and as we approached he fled to the edge of the precipice. He was constantly muttering to himself and twirling his beloved's battered lota. It was a remarkable exhibition of the force of love in the heart of a Mahratta."

"Do you think it is rare," asked Morgan, "to find such strength of affection in the hearts of the people of India?"

"No, I think not," replied the captain; "in fact, I think it quite common. We strangers from a colder climate, and a life which requires all of our time and faculties to get along in the world, do not understand how all the energies of this people are given to the training of the affections. I only realized it when I saw the devotion of my own dear Hindu wife. She had a power of loving never surpassed in this world, and it kindled within me such flames of love that every thought of her is precious to me even after the many years of her death. I smile sometimes at Dennis because of his antics prompted by his love for Kismut, but I am sure, if he once wins her love, he will never be unhappy when she is by his side; she will give him a wealth of affection that will bring blessedness into his life every day. O, how I miss my lost loved one!"

The captain then relapsed into silence for a while, and Morgan sat by his side, unwilling to break into his revery of grief. At length the captain said: "Morgan, let me tell you my story, and you will see why I so often lapse into silence or walk away from the jestings of my comrades. I came to India before the mutiny of 1857, and was established along the Ganges in command of a regiment of Sepoys. While there I became intimate with a Brahman whose sons were in my command. Of course, as a foreigner, I could not meet them in social life, but I often saw their little sister, a beautiful child, then not old enough to leave home for married life. When the mutiny broke out the father and sons fell, and I took the maiden with me, for she seemed at that time to have no one to care for her. I was attracted by her marvelous beauty, and as she grew older this beauty increased. As she grew to womanhood I taught her, and with ready capacity she learned until she knew as much as I did. Then I found myself unable to resist her charms, and with her full consent made her my wife. I then learned the depth of the affection a Hindu woman is capable of bestowing upon her beloved, and my life was one continual gleam of sunshine. Whenever she looked at me the love-light flashed in her eyes. She was constantly studying how to please me by little surprises, and when she saw me look back to her with love, she would sing and coo about me as if she knew nothing but love. She would not allow any other hand than her own to prepare my food, and it was always as choice as it could be made. Her caresses, her sweet words, her gentle sympathies, were the charm of life to me.

One day a little daughter came to us, and then our love was centered upon it; yet we loved each other none the less. The little child strongly resembled its mother, and in infantile manners seemed to catch her ways. One day—O, sad day to me!—I was ordered to report at Calcutta. With fond kisses and promises of a speedy return, I bade them farewell and departed. I hurried my return, and hastily leaving the railroad station, I rushed to my cottage, but it was empty. What did it mean? I went to my head-quarters, and there I was told my beloved wife had suddenly died and my child had disappeared. I made every effort to find my child and to discover the cause of my beloved's death, but all in vain. Then I asked to be relieved of my command. When the cause of my request was known I was sent to China with Gordon, and from there I went to Egypt, but my heart was in India. Unable to remain away any longer, I asked to be returned to India, and here I am. God only knows what the future of my life may be, but when I found my wife dead the light of my life faded, and the only spark of real hope left is that I may yet find a trace of my child."

While the captain was speaking his guest could hardly retain his seat or suppress his emotions, and at the close he said: "Captain Grey, believe me, God will yet bring your daughter to you. He will not permit such faith and love to go unrewarded."

The captain merely responded, "I hope so—I hope so," and, thanking his friend for his sympathy, retired to his room to prepare for the usual evening's drill of the garrison in the fortress.

With hurried step Morgan went down to the cottage, and long before he reached it Nemorama came out to meet him. O, how beautiful she looked as her eyes sparkled with love and she hastened to close the door, that she might receive his fond caresses and return them in like fervor! Looking into her fond eyes, he said: "Would my beloved be happy in seeing her own real father?" Nemorama instantly broke away from his embrace, and with a startled air quickly answered: "It has been the greatest desire of my life. I have thought of it every hour since you told me of my parentage. And now I see by your face that you know where he is. O, I am so happy! Where is he? shall I, O, may I see him soon?"

Then Morgan again drew her to him, and told her what he had just learned. The news was too good to keep, and Kismut was called in from the next room, and in her loving, quiet way was soon rejoicing with them. Nemorama was impatient to go to the fortress at once, but Morgan restrained her, for he was thinking of a plan by which he might have the revelation of hope fulfilled burst upon the captain at once.

After the parade Dennis came down. This was his usual practice now, and Kismut was never surprised at his coming, and they told him the news in store for his master. Dennis was very dignified when he came in. He always was so just after the parade, but he became entirely unconscious of self while the story was being told him. His face grew long, then it broadened; he smiled until every tooth was seen. Then the flushes spread and tears dropped from his eyes. He uttered the names of saints and all manner of exclamations, and finally wound up his strange behavior by embracing Morgan, then Kismut, before the others. Respect for the captain and for Morgan prevented him from serving Nemorama in the same way, but he refrained, and bowed low at her feet. He promised to keep quiet, however, and do his part in Morgan's plan to restore the daughter to her loving father.

CHAPTER XXVII.

THE LOST FOUND.

THE exodus of people from Bombay was filling every cottage on the mountains. Many of the people were compelled to bring tents, which they pitched in well-favored places, and enjoyed not only the change of climate and scenery, but also the change in their manner of living. The landscape became very attractive with the thousands of white tents on knolls and crags and beside the flowing streams.

The old fortress was a place of great interest to the visitors, and they never wearied of hearing the accounts of the exploits of Sejani, the Mahratta hero. Captain Grey was a typical English commander. He carried himself with great dignity, and had every thing pertaining to garrison work attended to with precision. He was just the kind of a man to lead people to say of him, "That man would die, but would not surrender; he has the true bull-dog grit." What would they have thought had they known how his heart was constantly bleeding because of the wounds of love?

Morgan had learned just exactly how the captain's wife was dressed when she bade him farewell, and he had secured for Nemorama an exactly similar suit.

When she donned it Morgan said she never had appeared lovelier—but he made the same remark every day. Nemorama showed possession of English blood by the impatience with which she awaited the time to make herself known. Kismut, however, full of sympathy, kept her mind upon trifles, changes of dress, added decorations to her hair, any thing to enable her to pass the time easily. Dennis had returned to the fortress. His work now was to prepare the way, to keep off intruders, and manage the captain should any trouble arise.

Captain Grey was sitting in his parlor reading the latest arrival of the *London Times*. His room was in perfect order—Dennis always kept it so. Every book was in its proper place on the shelves, the chairs were standing in their places as regularly as pickets on duty, the curtains at the windows were drawn just so far, to the half-inch, and the covers on the tables were spread so that the corners were precisely at equal distances from the floor.

The captain dropped the paper from his hand and fell to musing as the light grew dim and the darkness slowly came on. Dennis did not hurry with the lights. The captain was fond of these evening musings. It was the hour when his thoughts were with the departed one. His conversation with Morgan had opened the wounds afresh, and as the twilight faded a great lonesomeness came upon him. He was resting his head upon his hand and lost in thought when an unusual footstep was heard coming into the room. It was so soft, so gentle, that it was just noticeable, and that was all.

The captain aroused from his reverie. He knew it was a child or a woman's step; but how came either to be in his room? He looked up quickly, then leaped from his chair, turned pale, and, clasping his hands convulsively, asked the intruder, "For God's sake, tell me, who are you? Are you a spirit, or do you live?" Then he passed his hands to his head, as if in doubt whether he was in command of his senses or not. He saw before him, just as he had seen her years before, his beloved wife—the same face, the same dress, the same manner; and before the strange visitant could utter a word he burst into tears.

Then Nemorama quickly advanced, and putting out her warm, soft hand with a touch that thrilled him through and through, said, "Father, I am your daughter. Do you think I am like my dear, dead mother? Am I so much like her that you thought it was her spirit? Won't you welcome me, father, now that we have found each other?" Before she was done speaking he had folded her in his arms and was rapturously embracing her. He would hold her off at arm's-length and carefully scan her features, then with a cry of delight draw her to him again. Then, when able to command his feelings, he drew a chair beside his own, and bidding her be seated, asked her to tell him how she came to find him.

Hour after hour passed. The moon on her solemn march sent her beams through the window, lighting the apartment with her gentle touch; and the father and daughter talked of all the past. Both were inexpressibly happy. Neither of them doubted the truth of their relationship; and as they presented to each other the experiences through which they had passed, they rejoiced in the wonderful ways by which divine Providence had led them. Nemorama did not conceal her love for her preserver; and Captain Grey already loved Morgan as a son.

At length the captain touched the bell-cord, and in a moment Dennis, with his face radiant, stood before him. In another moment Morgan and Kismut entered, and the circle was complete. The captain, taking Morgan's hand, said:

"My dear friend, when I first met you on the steamer coming to India I felt a strange attraction to you, and since then I have had a yearning fondness for you. I did not know why. I was even surprised at it. But now it is all clear. You have been the means of bringing back to me in great measure my lost joy. In perils you have fought your way for love's dear sake, and you have won the victory. It is my first glad privilege in receiving my daughter to bestow her upon you. May she make you as happy as her mother made me! Only of one thing be assured. I shall never again be separated from my child. Lost once, she shall not be lost again until the time comes for one of us to go to the home above, where her dear mother awaits us."

Then he turned to Dennis, and, while the faithful fellow blubbered like a child, he said to him: "My true, faithful man, always ready to serve me, how can I repay you for your trustworthiness in all things placed in your hands? You are like a son to me. Without you I might not have received this blessing, and I can only say I rejoice in your service. I give you my confidence; and as you take Kismut as the 'darlint of yer heart,' may God bless you and make both of you to be supremely happy."

Then Dennis went out, and in a few moments returned with choice refreshments; and while they ate the cake and drank the lemonade they joyfully continued their touching life-narratives. It was nearly morning when they parted, but no one was allowed to leave the fortress, and Dennis had made abundant preparations to entertain them all.

In a few days there was a double wedding, and the old fortress was crowded with the guests who came from every cottage, nearly, on that mountain road. The Hindus, however, would have nothing to do with it. They abhorred the entire affair as an invention of evil ones. It was true both maidens had once been high caste, the one by right of inheritance and faithful life, the other by maternal inheritance alone; but both of them had lost caste by fellowshiping with those who were not of their caste, and also by failing to maintain the acts of purification demanded by their laws. To associate with them, gifted and noble though they were, would have been constant contamination and a denial of the eternal, binding power of their religion. The one hardship the women had now to suffer was the complete isolation from their sister Hindus. On the other hand, a new field for enjoyment opened before them.

Soon every English household in Bombay, as well as in the mountain resorts, knew the main incidents in the lives of the two heroines, who were lionized with the fullness of English enthusiasm. The beauty of Nemorama became the subject for universal praise, while the sweetness of disposition manifested by Kismut won a place in every heart. They had no time to bewail separation from their sisters of India because of the demands upon their time by their newly found sisters, and they realized that the liberty of the new life was like a heaven to their souls. O, how precious that freedom was to them!

When the first round of pleasure was ended, the cholera had subsided and the people were returning to their homes in Bombay. The ladies at the fortress began to consider seriously how they might consecrate their efforts to the elevation of their own people. They discovered that while Hinduism led people to be selfish in their duties, Christianity led people to be liberal, and awakened a desire within the heart to bring others into the same happy condition.

Mohammedanism was progressive, and, with tremendous energy, was winning converts all over India, but it was vastly different in its methods and promises from Christianity.

Mohammedanism held the most brilliant promises before men of the gratification of every form of sensual desire in the other world, and with stirring force appealed to the unregenerate and selfish natures of men. But Christianity appealed to the heart: it elevated the ideas of men; it led them into the desire for truth, virtue, and goodness. It taught men how to live right in this world, and, because of their right living, to be accepted in the kingdom of righteousness and dwell with their Saviour forever.

Kismut could testify that her allegiance to Christ did not antagonize any pure or virtuous thought she had ever known, but rather that it strengthened her desire for perfect purity. It sustained her in the endeavor to be faithful in all the obligations of life. It filled her mind with brighter and more certain assurances of eternal bliss, and it filled her soul with a joy that was a perpetual fountain, and not subject to the smiles or the frowns of any man. Beyond this it led her to look upon all women as sisters, whatever be their caste or condition, and to recognize in each one an immortal human soul.

With eager haste both of them began the study of the English language, determined to be able to read the Bibles of the English, and to glean from them the impressions which they observed in the conversation of those who surrounded them.

Day by day they were taught by their husbands, and, with their minds opened by love, were capable of rapid advancement. Morgan was surprised at the capacity for learning manifested by Nemorama. She seemed to grasp intuitively the ideas he presented, and she showed an eagerness that baffled fatigue.

He now brought the active powers of his trained mind to unfold truth to her, but, with all his intelligence, he found an inability to convey certain classes of impressions. Something more than mere knowledge was required. What was it?

As he pondered this question the fact of psychological differences between the sexes became the plainer to him, and the conviction arose that for a woman to receive a thorough training of her mental faculties she must be taught by a woman.

What an argument for the sustaining of woman's work in India!

He determined to test the matter by taking the ladies to Agra and placing them for a time under the influence of Mrs. Stanhope.

When he mentioned it they were willing, and immediately began their preparations. He assured them that all danger was now over; that neither fakir nor rajah could injure them, for the whole power of England would be used to defend the daughter and the wife of her officers.

CHAPTER XXVIII.

CHANGING SCENES.

RETURNING from the mountain sanitarium, the widow of Paul Stanhope laid down her grief at the Master's feet, and instead took up the work which he had placed before her. She labored with an energy that was sublime, and by day and by night hearkened to the calls of the poor and suffering. While giving them healing balms, she told them of the real balm of Gilead, the all-powerful love of the Saviour of sinners. The work grew on her hands, and she realized that in porportion to it she was like a single miner digging away at the base of a mighty mountain. Day by day she brought out precious ore, but a hundred thousand workers could work with her and still the great mountain would remain, so vast was the field.

Then she thought of the women of America, thousands of them given to a life of frivolity because there did not seem to be any cause before them to arouse and employ their best energies.

O the blindness of the women of America! God had taught them the sisterhood of the race; philology taught them the close sisterhood of the women in India; commerce taught them the sisterhood in tastes and provided the means of ready communication; and religion taught them the will of their Redeemer to accept the obligations of this sisterhood and go to work to carry the blessings of their faith and the freedom of the Gospel to them all. A revival of the missionary spirit was needed in America. Such a revival would be beneficial in many ways. It would arouse the people to a sense of their need of a Saviour; it would quicken the religious energies of the people accustomed to hearing the Gospel; it would stimulate all manner of missionary enterprise; it would open the windows of heaven for the outpouring of the divine blessing, and it would save the people of India. Such were the thoughts which often came in Mrs. Stanhope's mind.

Sometimes she wrote long, yearning, appealing letters home, telling the story of India's needs, but she spent more of her time in prayer that God would open the way before her to do his urgent work. She constantly met grave difficulties; it was so hard to win the people to positive action. She realized that whenever a high caste woman accepted Christ she was thoroughly ostracized by her former friends, and all she could call friends were the few in the missionary compound. Thus every high caste convert became a heroine for the Lord Jesus, and could truly say,

> "Naked, poor, despised, forsaken,
> Thou from hence my all shalt be."

It became to them a new life, with new hopes, new joys, new habits, and new associations.

Pitied or despised by former friends, the convert with a bleeding heart fled to Jesus and received grace sufficient for every time of need. One of the most difficult things to do was to take the pariah by the hand and say to her with loving kiss, "Thou art my sister."

Yet in the missionary compound there was not, there could not be, any recognition of caste. It was fundamentally opposed by all the doctrines of Christianity, and in the Scriptures were many expressions of the Lord's will condemning it.

Converts came slowly, and mostly from the pariahs or low-castes, and the very successes seemed to be barriers in the way of winning the high caste. But the faithful missionary pressed on her way. When Morgan arrived at the compound with Nemorama and Kismut they were received joyfully, and Morgan, with gladness in his heart, saw that Mrs. Stanhope looked up to him and loved him as a brother; and as he was impressed with this, he vowed to his own soul and to God that in all things he would be a faithful brother to her. He soon learned several things in regard to her trials and duties. First, he learned that she was overworked, and if she continued in that way she would soon be laid in the ground by the side of her husband. Then he discovered that the limited means at her disposal were insufficient to enable her to carry on her work, except at a constant sacrifice of little pleasures greatly needed by herself as recreation and stimulation. Then he saw that she was painfully burdened by the indifference of her sex in America to the needs of missionary work. She was toiling with strained energies while they were at ease in Zion.

He thought, "The missionary leads a hard life, and when the people at home fail in their support it becomes crushing." His coming was the gleaming of the sunshine to her wearied soul, and she yielded to his earnest importunities to divide her time. So much for work, so much for rest.

Nemorama and Kismut became her students, and Morgan was soon convinced that his theory was correct. They learned from a woman phases of truth, ways of grasping things, methods of study, and illumination of doctrines such as he, because he was a man, could not convey to them. It was now plain to his mind that the theory underlying woman's work in India for woman was not a mistake, but a great fact. And he determined to consecrate a large proportion of his income to sustaining this work. Every day he drove around the beautiful gardens of Agra, accompanied by the ladies, and the bloom gradually came to the cheeks of the missionary, and her manners becamo sprightly as in her early life. They were all happy, and the days quickly sped away. One day a message came to him, telling of the illness of his father, and bidding him hasten his return. The message had come on the wings of the telegraph, and only a few hours after it was sent from New York it reached him in Agra. He immediately telegraphed to Bombay to learn the time for the departure of the next steamer for England. The answer came, and he had but one day more to spend in Agra. Their plans were soon made. Kismut would return to the fortress. The captain would meet them in Bombay. Mrs. Stanhope would go to Bombay to see them off, then to the fortress for a rest of a few days, and Nemorama would accompany her husband to America. One more ride to the Taj, and then farewell. As they were riding along a group of people by the road-side attracted their attention. It was an ordinary spectacle. A holy fakir was sitting at his devotions, and the passers-by were worshiping him. As they drew near Morgan glanced at the holy man, and at once recognized his deliverer.

Stopping his horses and bidding a cooly attend to them, he leaped to the ground and assisted Nemorama to alight, telling her as he did so that this holy man had been the means of restoring her to her father and delivering her lover from prison. With their usual courtesy the crowd gave way before the white gentleman and lady. For several moments no motion was made by the fakir. His eyes were closed, and he seemed to be as fixed as a statue. Morgan saw how his emaciation had increased, and he now looked like a living skeleton. The people were uttering in low tones their admiration of the exceedingly holy man, and every face was expressive of adoration.

The tears flowed down Nemorama's cheeks, and at length, unable to further control her emotion, she knelt in front of him, and taking hold of his bony, claw-like hand, pressed her lips to it again and again. It was a strange sight, at least so thought a company of tourists who, passing by, stopped to observe the scene. Youth, beauty, and grace honoring a gross animal-like form of a man, a half-naked, matted-haired, starved, unwashed, insane-looking being, while the American husband of the woman stood calmly looking on. Morgan saw no impropriety in it. He knew the fakir was thoroughly sincere in his faith, and as true as man could be. As he watched his wife he too could not restrain the tears, for he thought of the suffering the fakir had endured in order to accomplish the generous work of which he, a stranger, had reaped the benefit. The woman's affection at length aroused the fakir, and opening his eyes, he saw the party before him. A tender smile broke over his face, and taking his other hand from its usual place of repose, placed it on the woman's head and blessed her.

The crowd of Hindus about them would have given all they were worth for such a blessing, and they were amazed to see it bestowed upon one in the dress of a foreigner. The fakir then motioned Morgan to approach, and when he had come to him, said, as he took from his matted hair two bullets and handed them to him, "The Mohammedan thought these were mighty charms, and hoped by possessing them to be able to accomplish all he desired. He was patient, and succeeded in some things, but I met him in the castle cell after the American had escaped from prison and death. We fought each other until death seized upon him; then I took the bullets from his hair to restore them to their owner. The gun that shot them is laid up as a trophy in the rajah's hunting castle. The stranger is brave and good, and has found the father of the maiden, and has made her his wife. The fakir is now content, his life-work is done; he will henceforth know no human being, but while a few days are left him will be absorbed with thoughts of Brahm. Take this gem: whenever you look upon it, let a prayer rise from your heart for the fakir who never lost sight of you when you were working out the destiny of one of the chosen daughters of the Hindu race."

He then handed Morgan the ruby with the mystical letters engraved upon it, and immediately folding his arms again, closed his eyes, and was apparently unconscious of all about him.

Morgan helped Nemorama into the carriage, and they drove on to the Taj. They walked through the beautiful gardens, entered the charming tomb, lunched in the spacious rest-house, loitered by the founatins, and after hours of feasting, their souls with the beauty about them re-entered their carriage, and quickly drove toward Agra. As they passed the place where they had seen the fakir, they looked and beheld him still there, sitting absolutely motionless. As they continued on their way, Nemorama said to her companion, "He may never stir again, but sit there in that solemn repose until life departs from sheer exhaustion, and the people will say of him, 'The holy fakír has gone to Brahm.'"

Early the next morning the travelers entered the cars to hasten to Bombay. They stopped in the city only long enough to make a few purchases, and then hastened to the steamer. Captain Grey had obtained leave of absence, and was ready to accompany them. The parting with Dennis was a severe trial to him, they had been companions for so many years. Nemorama wept as she embraced Kismut for the last time, for she had learned to love her more than any other woman in India. But for no one was the parting more trying than for Morgan as he said farewell to Mrs. Stanhope. He felt as if a part of his life-work was to watch over her and aid her in her work. But the partings were soon over, and the great vessel, amid the cheers of the crowds on the quay, began the voyage to England.

In thirty days the travelers reached New York. Edward Morgan arrived at home in time to present his wife to his father, and after the dying man had carefully scanned her countenance, he said to his son,

"My boy, your wife is beautiful and good; she will crown your life with happiness. And now kneel, both of you, and receive my blessing before I die." As soon as the funeral was over, Nemorama bent her every energy to learning more perfectly the English language, determined, when she mastered it, to go forth to tell the women of America publicly and privately of the sufferings endured by the women of India because of the social bondage of Brahmanism, and to urge them in the name of the blessed Saviour to sustain woman's work for woman in India, until every zenana should be opened to Christ and every bound soul be made free.

THE END